Risk

A Novel

Mark Victor Young

Copyright

Risk by Mark Victor Young

Published by **Hanton House Creative Media** in London, Canada.

ISBN: 978-0-9938558-3-2

First print edition October 2014

Enquiries: HHCreativeMedia@icloud.com

Cover Designed by Christina Young at http://christinalorraineyoung.com/

—

Risk

The Loss

Martin Porchnik could see Jason from Claims approaching the Underwriting area with a yellow file in his hand and a big smirk on his face. A chill went through Martin, as it always did. A yellow file meant a property claim to be paid, and although he would ask not for whom the bell tolled, he still prayed it didn't toll for he.

"Good afternoon, 'Underwear' department. Whose day can I ruin today?" said Jason. "Anybody have a file for Ultimate Diecasting?"

Martin grimaced. He knew that name. Of all the shit files that landed in his lap, that one stuck out in his memory as one of the shittiest.

"Heads are going to roll over this one," said Jason, looking around with an evil grin.

"Not one of mine," said Darlene.

"It's not me," called Dave from his cubicle at the back.

"It's me," said Martin. Everybody looked at him and he shrugged his shoulders. What're ya gonna do?

"Is this the kind of crap you're writing down here?" Jason parked his bulk next to Martin's desk, leaning his elbow on the upper shelf. "No wonder I'm so busy paying out the big bucks. I need a dec page, underwriter boy."

He was what might be called a *big galoot*. Tallish and stocky going on fat with dark curly hair and thick eyebrows that looked angry or at least sarcastic all the time and a kind of goatee that made him look devilish.

"I haven't even issued the policy, yet," Martin said, looking away from Jason's dark eyes and back down at the yellow file that spelled possible doom. Did he have to enjoy it so much?

"Well, what's the hold up? Let's get it in gear. Do I have to come down here and crack the whip on you people?"

"It just came in last week." He dug through his pile of bound submissions waiting to be entered into the computer.

"Well, that didn't take long. What have you got for me, so I know how much I have to pay out here? Or did you want me to just give them a blank check?"

"We have a copy of their last year's dec page from the prior carrier. We bound coverage on the same basis." Well, he hadn't, but his boss had. The decs, or policy declarations, which were a listing of the coverages and wordings included, had just landed in his lap, in fact. And right away he had to hand them over to Jason so he could pay the first claim. Delightful.

"Gee, thanks. I guess it's something to go by. I'll make a copy, then."

"Can you leave me the claim file?"

"Sure. Read it and weep." Jason passed him the file and then walked away to the mail room to make his photocopy.

"Believe me, there will be tears," said Martin. He opened the file with a small feeling of self-satisfaction that he hoped wouldn't show on his face. He wasn't the one who had put them on the risk, so the blame wouldn't fully fall to him, come to that. It gave him a little get-out-of-jail-free card, but it was something he had to pretend he didn't think.

Underwriters spend most of every day considering risk. They read submissions of potential "risks," which in his department were businesses they were asked to insure. They had to assess the likelihood of having to pay out money because of some misadventure that might befall each. This would be some kind of lawsuit or a fire or a flood, etc. If you included famine, you would have almost all four horsemen of the Apocalypse. War is excluded. Underwriters choose which businesses to insure and how much money to charge so that, on average, a certain class of business would make money for the company.

The general principle of insurance is that the premiums of the many pay for the losses of the few. So they wrote up business for a whole lot of machine shops across Canada and only a few, like Ultimate Diecasting, would have a claim, and it should all even out and whatever was left over minus expenses was profit. If Martin did his job right.

So that is most of what underwriters do: consider which risks to get and which ones to keep by renewing. The rest of what they do all day is worry that the risks they have selected will have a big claim and they will be hauled onto the mat to answer for it. Consider risk and worry for a living. Nice work if you can get it. Martin shook his head and tried to concentrate on the claim report.

The date of loss was Sunday, so it had been the previous night. It was a professional hit. The line to the alarm monitoring station had been cut and the bars had been taken out along with the window, which was removed in one piece from the frame. The place was a mess and the only things missing were plans and blueprints from a current job. There would be a payout under "Valuable Papers" and a Business Interruption loss while the plans were reassembled. They would have to pay to have the line repaired and the window replaced. Nothing else stolen or destroyed. That didn't sound right.

This one had disaster written all over it from the start. He remembered when the phone call had come in from the broker, only a week ago, and it hadn't passed the sniff test from the start.

"Hi, Martin. Listen, I've got a piece of new business for you. It's a machine shop. Do you think you could do it for four thousand bucks?"

"Let me take a look at it. Put some details on paper and fax it over."

"Can't you just quote me over the phone?"

"Well, what do they make?"

"Just various metal products."

"It makes a difference to what we would charge. And I'll also need construction and protection details on the building to determine the property rate."

"It's HCB, steel deck roof, of course. What else? I'm a busy man, Martin. I don't have time to get into all this detail."

"I can't quote over the phone. I'll need something in writing. Including receipts. Do they sell to the U.S.?"

"What do you think? Everybody sells to the U.S. This is just a little risk, I don't see the big deal."

"Sales to the U.S. increases our exposure. You'd better send something over."

"I'll get back to you."

Unbelievable, was his first thought when he had hung up the phone. What do we even need underwriters for if that's the way we're going to deal in insurance? It's not about the size of the building they occupy, or the number of people they have working for them, their level of training and qualification, or who they sell their products to, or how much they sell, or how much equipment they have and what it costs to replace it, would a key piece of equipment shut down the whole shop while it was being repaired, or whether they deal in cash or credit, or how long a fire would put them out of business, or ten or fifty other things that Jed Johansen wouldn't think to ask... it's about a few thousand bucks and a quick sale. Granted, 99% of brokers were diligent and professional and trustworthy, but it was the ones like

Jed Johansen that you had to watch or else you ended up in situations like the one he was currently facing.

Jed never did send in a full quote submission, he just went over Martin's head and spoke to Gerry. "Gerry" was short for Geraldine, his supervisor. She preferred the diminutive, as she didn't live in the Victorian age. She was tall and confident and blond, and Martin found her easier to deal with than his previous boss. She had an intelligent face and sharp eyes. She was impatient all the time, but kind. From looking at the pictures on the desk of her husband and kids, he imagined she was one of those busy moms who were great with their kids, efficient at work and able to keep the whole world spinning on the end of a stick.

"I just got off the phone with one of the Johansen brothers, I forget which," Gerry had said when she dropped by his desk not twenty minutes after the first phone call came through. "I bound that risk, the machine shop, for $5000. He's faxing over last year's dec page."

"Oh," he had said hesitantly. This was very bad form, indeed. Without a written submission, there were no declarations or representations from the broker upon which to rely, and as they say, a verbal contract isn't worth the paper it's printed on, ha-ha.

"I know," said Gerry. "You're not happy about it."

Martin shrugged but looked steadily at her. "Not really. I don't like him bypassing me to get to you. You can't be doing all the quotes in the department."

"I know. It was an accommodation. This is a

growth year, and we have got to take it where we can get it. Besides, we can get it inspected and take care of any problems then."

"When it will be too late to get more premium if we need it."

"It'll be fine, Martin. Besides, we're $5K to the good, instead of nothing, and I want to switch the Johansens on so they'll start sending us more business."

"I understand."

Five thousand dollars? They knew nothing about security, products, contracts, warranties... it would have to be inspected, thought Martin, just as the fax had been dropped off in his IN box.

It was out in Scarberia, their nickname for Scarborough, the north east part of Toronto. It was in a moderately high crime area, big limits on tools and computers, which were the first to go. This was terrible. The Total Insured Value, or TIV, was over $4 million: the company's money on the line for who knows what. And now a claim, proving him right about his fears.

"Here's your so-called dec page back." Jason loomed by his desk again. "Can I have my file back, or were you going to take it home with you?"

"It's all yours. Why do you think thieves would break into a place like that and not steal any tools or computers? Things with a quick turn around. Those are usually the first to go, and yet these thieves ignored them."

"What do you think, oh brainy one?"

"I think they knew what they were looking for. All they took was highly specialized diagrams, plans, and design specs. What petty thief takes that?"

"Okay, so what?"

"It sounds suspicious, that's all. I think you should be careful with this one. It's bothered me since we wrote it."

"Well, thanks for the advice. I'm glad you know so much about how to do my job, because you obviously didn't know how to do yours."

"Hey, it was just a suggestion."

"I'll take it under advisement," said Jason over his shoulder.

When the adjuster had left, Martin quickly composed a fax form and fired it off to the broker: *Urgent. Insist that the insured upgrades security system to provide ULC-approved Line Security Level III protection, to prevent a recurrence of this kind of loss. Please advise ASAP how the insured intends to proceed. Our file is in abeyance pending your reply.* Then he walked over and knocked on Gerry's door.

"I know what you're going to say. I heard about it."

"I'm not going to say anything. I'm just wondering about this loss. It sounds suspicious to me. No tools or computers stolen. I still don't think we've got the whole story here, and that could mean non-disclosure. In which case we could VOID the policy *ab initio.*"

"Marty. Get a grip. Bad losses happen to good underwriters. It's not your fault, and I know that.

Leave the investigation to the Claims Department."

"Okay. I faxed the broker to get the line security in there or else face the hammer."

"That's all we can do. Now blow it off. You've had bigger losses than this. Besides, it builds character."

"It builds my stress level is what it does."

Leaving Gerry to her managing, he returned to his cube feeling dissatisfied. It was a mystery, that was for sure. But if he were reading this mystery in one of his detective novels, he would've put it down by now. Too boring. Something about this was not right, but it wasn't really his place to intrude. Let the Claims Department do their work. They were thorough, Jason's bluster notwithstanding. If there was something to find, they'd find it. Time to shake this off with a little caloric input.

He sat in the lunchroom quietly munching his sandwich. People came and went, mostly going back to eat at their desks, or going out for lunch. Martin was a fixture in the lunchroom: same time, same lunch, everyday. Lunch was about giving his mind a break. No magazines or TV, no conversation, no stimuli. It wasn't a Zen thing: be the sandwich, one hand clapping, or whatever. It just felt good to decompress and not think about anything, if he could manage it. Concentrate on the flavor of the sandwich and the chocolate bar.

It was the chocolate bars that gave him the spare tire, he felt, but he couldn't stop. They were an addiction. He was about 5'10", pudgy, especially around the gut. The old hairline was slowly

retreating on him. At 38 years old, this was right on
schedule, par for the genetic course. Thanks,
Grandpa. But it didn't help that the media was
always bombarding women with images of the ideal
male, an ideal he couldn't live up to. Calvin Klein
underwear ads had set his self-esteem back a pace, he
could admit it now.

He poured another cup of coffee and went back to
the cube. He tried to get back into the flow of things,
but the stupid loss kept bugging him and he ended
up just staring off into space for long periods of time,
just trying to crack the code of this puzzle. That was
how George, the bicycle courier who did their head
office mail run every day found him, lost in thought
at his desk.

"Hey, buddy," he said, picking up the name plate
on his desk and flipping it over in his hand, tapping it
on the desk. "Where's my envelope?"

"Hey, go easy on the name plate."

"Sorry about that. I don't want to break the last
link to your sense of identity."

"Don't worry, my name's sewn into the backs of all
my shirts."

"There you go. You'll be fine."

"All right, just let me collect it up." Martin got up
out of his chair, glad for something else to think
about and a chance to shoot the breeze with George.
He had been doing the pick-ups at their office for a
few years now and he and Martin had been out for
drinks a couple of times after work. He was a good
guy, despite his scary appearance. Tall, sunglasses,

white man's dreadlocks, tattoos, pierced this and that... he wasn't like Martin's insurance friends, but that's what he liked about him. He was different.

"No rush. I'm ahead of schedule today," said George.

George came with him into the mail room, and talked to him as he gathered up all the envelopes, memos, and various other correspondence, packaged and weighed it all, and wrote out the receiving slip.

"So, rough day, or just hungry?" said George.

"It's been one of those days. Started out okay, but it all went quickly downhill this afternoon."

"Sounds like a pretty normal Monday."

"Yeah, I guess. Well, here it is. Signed, sealed, and now just to be delivered."

"Thanks. We going for drinks tonight, Marty?"

"Not tonight, but maybe some night this week."

"Just say the word." George put on his sunglasses as Martin walked him out through the office and over to the main door.

"Bye, George," called Janice.

"Bye." The door closed behind him.

"Whew, he's cute," said Janice. "Do you know if he's single?"

"Um, yes. I mean, yes, I do know he lives with his girlfriend."

"Too bad. Such a hottie! He can deliver my package anytime."

Janice was a bit of a hottie herself, in that secretary way. Single secretaries exude this air of availability and eagerness, like bridesmaids. She was no supermodel, which Martin didn't mind. That type of woman intimidated Martin, anyway. They always looked so severe, so hard, with angry-looking cheek bones. He always imagined them as martial arts experts, capable of knocking his block off if he so much as looked at them.

No, she was solidly built, pretty, and seemed fun to be around. Shoulder length blond hair-product hair, small features, fair-sized bust and hips. Looking very fertile. In her early 30's, he guessed. But she would probably say no. Look at him. Why would she go out with him? He wasn't much to look at. And even if they did go out once or twice, something would happen and the whole thing would go to hell and it would hurt like the last time he got involved with someone. Then he wouldn't be able to look her in the eye at work the next morning. Always have to pretend to check out the paint job on the walls as he walked by her desk. And face the shame of a failed office romance. It wasn't worth it.

Quietly back across the office, shy glance around, wishing he could turn himself invisible, wanting to escape people's notice and make it back to the safety of his little cube without anyone confronting him. Feeling strangely persecuted, as if everyone were against him. Couldn't seem to face anything or anyone right now.

The Courier

When George threw a leg over the cross bar and popped his toes into the clips, he felt like the bike became a part of him, part of his movements, the smooth motion of his legs compelling his forward momentum in a way he now found more natural than walking. A low tech cyborg. He positively flew on the longish trip north, his powerful legs carrying him faster than all the six-cylinders-in-V-formation, power-of-two-hundred-horses metal monsters lined up every block from Front Street to the 401 along Yonge Street, the trunk of the tree that grew into the longest street in the world.

Passing Bloor Street, Rosedale, the three long, slow inclines of "heartbreak hill" leading up to the Chum FM radio building, and then on past St. Clair to the long stretch of greenery in the Mount Pleasant Cemetery, finally pulling up for a red light at Davisville Avenue.

Catching his breath a bit, he stood on the pedals, balancing the bike and looking up ahead at the giant triangular neon strawberry on top of the Canadian Tire building across from his destination, and thought about ten floors of white-collar desk jockeys pledging daily allegiance to that symbology — in the elevators, on every door, on their business cards and letterhead, and on their paychecks. Chuckling to himself at this foolishness, he put his legs to the task at the turning of the light, and took off bearing north again, pulling up in less than a minute outside 2161 Yonge Street. He locked up the bike and took the seat with him onto the elevator to the 7th floor. Opened the double doors and announced himself.

"Courier."

"Oh, just a second," said yet another receptionist. "I'll get it."

George stood by the reception desk. The office slaves were giving him the surreptitious once and then twice over. He cut a dashing figure in his courier get-up, and he was used to turning heads. The bicycle shorts and zip front shirt were skin tight, and left little to the imagination. You got used to having your wobbly bits on display. Besides, he was in fantastic shape from all the riding and he collected stickers and buttons from all the offices that he visited and displayed them on the strap of his satchel, which was emblazoned with the logo, "Matrix Messenger Service."

"Here you go. 385 King Street East, as fast as you can go."

"If you'll just sign here." On with the Ray-Bans. Had to have the shades if you didn't want to get bugs in your eyes. "Thanks." Out the door. On the bike.

It wasn't about the money, which was shit. It

wasn't entirely an aversion to the office or even factory environment, although that was part of it. It was all about this, the wind in his hair, the bike... this feeling.

For the trip south, he decided to do the Gothics tour along Church Street, since it was on the way. He pushed east along Soudan, and then south on Mount Pleasant, past the rear gates of the cemetery, along past St. Clair, and then riding the pedals all the way down the hill past the David A. Balfour Park, onto Church and then continued south.

First the beautiful "Bishop's Palace" rectory just after Dundas with its awkward third story added like an afterthought 50 years after the main building was finished. Then the back of St. Michael's Cathedral and its "Victorian Gothic" cruciform shape. Onward then, to beautiful Met United, the "Cathedral of Methodism" in the High Victorian Gothic style, 1875 approximately. The last church on his mini tour was at his turn onto King Street: the St. James "Cathedral Church" and its single, massive, 300-foot-high tower and spire—the tallest steeple in Canada, designed by architects Thomas Ridout and F.W. Cumberland round about 1850. He tried to imagine how it must have looked when the majestic spires of these churches dominated the skyline, when the scale of buildings was low.

Then, as if the city knew he needed a break from all the gloomy Gothics, there was the exuberant St. Lawrence Hall and all the feathers, swords, and bugles you could imagine. William Thomas, 1850's,

Renaissance style. The names of these architects were like childhood heroes from bubble gum trading cards. All of it seeming so long ago now.

He stopped in front of 385 King, locked up his bike, and made the delivery.

After the last drop of the day, he retired to his favorite watering hole. It was a biker bar on Temperance Street, which is to say, bike courier bar. They all hung out there with their bikes leaning up against the patio railings, trees, and the walls of stores nearby. The shit was shot, tired limbs rested up on the tables, and they all partook of libations care of the fermented grape, sour mash, barley and hops. Except for George.

"Pellegrino. No ice."

"Oh, sure. Do you want that with a twist?" said Big Eddy.

"Yeah, how about a twist of bite me."

"Awww, tough day, honey?"

"When isn't it? The time I waste standing around, waiting for people to put things in envelopes. Meanwhile, the radio's buzzin' with other pickups."

"Boo-hoo," agreed Eddy. There were two Eddy's: Big and Little. Little Eddy was actually the taller of the two, but rail thin and quiet... a.k.a. Long John Sliver. Big Eddy, on the other hand, was built like a fire hydrant: short, but a physically-imposing specimen. He was all biceps, pecs, deltoids, and no neck. His thighs were like two big paint cans, both from the riding and the working out. He always wore a World Gym t-shirt, but despite the "dumb jock" appearance, he was actually quite intelligent, and was the undisputed leader of the group.

Chet broke in then to one-up him. "Oh, poor you. I had another knockdown today. Cabbie, of course. Bastard didn't even stop."

Nobody had more knockdowns than Chet, but whether this was the cause or result of his utter stupidity was always up for discussion. Everyone craned their necks to admire the fresh cuts and abrasions.

"Whoeee. Gonna need a skin graft?"

"That's some scrape."

"Why are cyclists invisible to cabbies?"

"Don't forget to save any medical bills for your taxes."

"Are you always this much of a weenie, Frank?"

"Save them for his lawyer, more like. Did you get the plate?"

"Hey, he'll thank me come tax time."

When they all had a drink, George proposed the nightly toast. "Gentlemen, let's charge our glasses to the deity who preserves us and keeps us safe from harm, keeps body and soul together, a shield against the cabbies, the pot holes, the sewer grates, and the bloody tourists walking against the lights.

"To fleet-footed Hermes, Messenger of the Gods."

"To Hermes," they all agreed.

After Work

Martin loosened his tie and stepped out the door onto the Yonge Street sidewalk, walking north in the late afternoon sunshine, enjoying the breeze, and trying to imagine how good it felt to be George, riding around all day in this beautiful city. He walked up Yonge Street past the Eaton Centre, where two sidewalk drummers were putting on a show for the rush hour crowd. Crazy pamphleteers and religious zealots shouted about redemption and shook leaflets or bibles in people's faces. As he crossed Dundas, he passed the man with the huge goiter on his neck.

"Eff you be-leaf in Jee-zuss Kuh-riced, you weel not pay-rish in Hal, but have eturr-nal life. Jee-zuss ees the own-lee way to Hay-vun. There ees no other way."

The guy was there at 5 o'clock every day without fail. Amazing resolve to convert the sinners. And then there was the "True Face of God" guy out front of The Gap, holding up books with a picture of an emaciated space alien on the cover. *As if we don't have enough problems with the gods we've got.* Past Sam the

Record Man and all the chess boys doing battle on
the concrete tables on Gould Street; past College, and
all the way up to the used bookstore district near
Wellesley. The usual route.

Despite his resolve to leave work at the office, he
couldn't help thinking about the details of that loss
on Ultimate Diecasting. Although it was forced on
him, he still felt a sense of responsibility for the
outcome. It was his file, now, and something wasn't
right about it. Either the loss was suspicious, or what
they knew about the risk itself was incomplete.
Neither situation was acceptable. As an underwriter,
all he could do was investigate the details of the
business and its products by ordering an inspection
of the premises or by questioning the broker. He had
to rely on Jason to investigate the claim.

Sometimes he felt like the Claims Department had
a mindset of "just pay" the claims without
questioning their legitimacy, because paying claims is
what they do. Not that they shouldn't pay legitimate
claims, but there will always be a small percentage of
claims presented which are in some way fraudulent
or inflated. Or simply not covered. That was where
the investigation part came in. They had a duty to all
policyholders not to incur costs from baseless claims
that would make everybody's rates go up. But he had
to leave that duty of care to Jason, the big lummox.
What else was he going to do, investigate it himself?

He had to shake off these thoughts and enjoy his
walk. The first stop after work every day was at one
of several used bookstores for a paperback novel.

Either a detective story or a police procedural, sometimes a western, even less frequently sci-fi. Once in a great long while he would choose a Romance novel of some sort, even though it created a painful longing sensation. Or resulted from a painful longing, who knows. Then over to the Brewer's Retail near Bloor for a six pack — always domestic because they were cheaper, but sometimes lager, other times ale, depending on his mood. Never a stout, though. He was stout enough.

Then he'd fight his way into the Bloor subway station and ride the Rocket back to the 'burbs with the other sardines. Off at Finch station, and walk the few blocks to his apartment. Up the elevator to the 9th floor.

When he had first looked at the building, he'd made sure to request an apartment on one of the first ten floors. Above that, the balconies were inaccessible to the fire department ladders and you would have to jump into that little circle of tarp. *Not this fat bastard, thank you very much.* He would put a hole in their tarp and end up in a crater with his lung punctured by his femur.

The construction of the building was fire-resistive: concrete floors, walls, and roof, all with a minimum two-hour fire rating, and a monitored fire-detection system. The little metal noses of the sprinkler system were visible poking through the ceiling every ten feet and Martin found them very comforting. There were two emergency stairs with fire alarm pull-stations, one at each end of the hallway, and both were within the correct minimum distance of every unit described by the code. He had checked. There was a standpipe and hose on every floor, and a smoke detector in every unit. Martin also had his own fire extinguisher.

From his selection of microwaveable frozen dinners, he chose "Salisbury Steak with Potatoes au gratin" and gave it a thorough nuking. He then untied his silk inverted hangman's noose and removed his other office attire in favor of his pajamas. After retrieving his dinner, a beer, and his paperback, "Double Dealing at the 87th Precinct", he settled into his easy chair for the evening.

Three hours later, he turned the last page of his book and somewhat blearily had the last swig of his sixth and final beer. He closed the cover, stood up and stretched. Only 10:30pm. Gathering up the chocolate bar wrappers, putting the book on his shelf, putting the six pack of empty bottles in his storage closet on top of a stack of ten others... it would soon be time to make a bottle return run. He rubbed his stomach thoughtfully. Maybe it wasn't just the chocolate bars; maybe a partial beer belly? Well, chocolate or beer, he wasn't likely to quit either.

He moved to the bedroom, sat on the bed, opened the bottom drawer of his bureau, and began to survey his collection of pornography in hopes of selecting a fetching beauty for the evening's masturbation. As a practicing single male, he was limited in his choice of sexual outlets. He had been to strip clubs in search of stimulation, but found it an awkward social situation when the "dancers" would try to engage him in conversation in hopes of relieving him of some private dance money. He couldn't hack it. The same reluctance, as well as a fear of other risks, extended to prostitution.

So that left him with his magazines. His few experiences with dating and girlfriends had also had an element of this awkwardness, so they had never come to… fruition, he liked to say. So that left him, at thirty-eight years old, step right up ladies and gentlemen, no crowding at the front there, you'll scare the freak, here he is, the oldest Canadian virgin.

Dinner Out

Because it was Monday they were both too tired to cook, so George and Gina went out for dinner. There were so many cafés and restaurants to choose from that they rarely ate at the same place twice. They would often walk miles from home to find somewhere to eat. Most restaurants had several menu selections catering to vegetarians, so they didn't usually have a problem.

"Mmm. Georgey, try this. It's delicious."

"Mmm. Good. Have a taste of this soup. This is the stuff."

"Oh, why didn't I have that? You want to trade?"

"No way! Hands off!"

"Suck. So Anderson finally offered me a promotion today. He said there was no money in the budget for raises, so I could have a lovely token promotion instead. Same job, same money, just a better title. Like this is going to help pay the rent."

"What a smug little weasel he is. As if he doesn't know that the job market is tough right now. You should shop around, anyway, just in case. It'd be so nice to shove a resignation in his face."

"It's not only tough, it's impossible. Look at you, still slingin' envelopes after all these years."

"What's wrong with that? I like it." George took a sip of his drink to cool his mouth. How did their conversation take this turn? Again.

"You haven't even tested the water since you took this job. You'd think you'd at least fire off your resumé once in awhile. Or have you given up on that course altogether?"

"I don't know. It's just not an option right now."

"Well, what about something else? You can't stay a courier all your life. If the architect thing isn't going to happen, why not try something else?"

"Something that paid a little better?"

"No, that's not what I mean. I don't care, really. But something that lets you use your brains, and yes, maybe make a little more money in the long run. That's not such a bad thing."

"Maybe I should just go schleppe around some factory, or become one of these office slaves I see every day. Get some faceless McJob?"

"That's not your only option. You're university-educated."

"In a field that's all full up, thank you very much. Not taking any new applications, there's the door, don't let it hit you in the ass on the way out."

"But tell me you don't care that this job has no future. Do you see yourself doing it in five years, or ten? Is that what you want? 'Cause if you can tell me that, I'll shut up right now. 'Nuff said. I just want you happy."

He said nothing.

"What about that offer your brother made you?"

"Let's just drop it."

Gina rolled her eyes. "Whatever." She was so beautiful when she was fed up with him. She had a great angry hair flip that spoke volumes and when she turned her dark brown eyes away from him and pursed those lips, he knew he was dismissed. That hair looked fantastic but took up huge amounts of her time and effort with various products, relaxers, straighteners, conditioners, hair spray and emergency salon visits. He thought it all unnecessary, as her worst hair crisis looked gorgeous anyway, but don't be telling a black woman about her hair. That is her own twisted love-hate relationship to manage by herself, with frequent consultations with her mother and various friends and stylists.

From the time they first met in university, her mischievous smile and, it had to be said, tight little figure, had him hooked. They were a bit of an odd couple: he was tall, she was not so tall; kinda nerdy guy, hip chick; he an architect in training, she an English major and secret poet... but both in love from the start. He thought of her as a Jada Pinkett-Smith and he was a Will Smith without the great pecs, Caucasian style.

He was 24 when he graduated with his degree in Architecture. He had hit every firm in town with his resumé, was the eager young kid: "Just take me on at any level and let me prove myself. I'll sweep the floors to start if I have to." But his timing was bad, because the economy had just nose-dived into a recession, and nobody was hiring. He couldn't even volunteer as an architect. And the floors were already being swept, thanks anyway, but they did need someone to do deliveries for the various architect firms around town. Rush deliver plans and blueprints from all the offices to their clients. Kind of like a bicycle courier. And who knows what it may lead to...

What it led to was more courier jobs. For a few years he made some half-hearted attempts to make the rounds with his resume again, but eventually he just gave it up. He was a courier, and that was it. He even liked the job. Loved the freedom of bombing around on his bicycle in the middle of the day while all his former classmates were stuck up in the concrete towers, sweating it out over deadlines.

"What about some dessert?" Gina asked, breaking the silence.

He smiled at the welcome segue. "I think I could handle it."

After dessert they had a leisurely walk home as the stars began to appear. They had been together since second year. Gina had graduated with her honors English degree, and got a job at an ad agency as a copywriter almost right away. They had talked about marriage a few times, but nothing was ever decided upon. Why bother, unless you were having a kid? And parenthood, if it was on the horizon, seemed a long way off.

The Screw Up

Mr. Smith gripped the bridge of his nose between thumb and forefinger and sighed. He opened his eyes to stare across the table at his two associates in apparent disbelief.

"That's every plan that was in the drawers, I told ya that already."

Mr. Smith spoke at last, although it was an effort to remain calm. "These are plans for major appliances. Do you think our client wants to build a better refrigerator?"

"That's where ya said to look. Am I some kind of mind reader?"

"You didn't even take a look at what it was you were stealing?"

"Jesus H. Christ, Harry, help me out here."

"When ya in a place illegally, it behooves ya to get outta there, like, expeditiously?"

"And not sit around reading blueprints."

"Well, next time you'll have to be more careful."

"Next time, what now?"

"Tomorrow night. Same place. You will need to break in again before they upgrade the security. I will make contact with our source and gather some more information."

"You want us to hit it again? That's a first."

"Isn't that kinda risky?"

"With what we're paying you, you will be well compensated. If you can get the job done."

"Hey, don't worry about it, we'll get the job done, like always. Just tell me it's gonna be worth it. What's the contract for?"

"Let that be of no concern to you. You'll be paid your usual rates in good time. And there will be a bonus if there's no police involvement."

"And who's the buyer? Ya still haven't told us that."

"Who cares, I say, as long as they got the dough."

"I still wanna know."

"The buyer is a highly motivated party with a lot of money. There's nothing else that you need to know about him. Suffice it to say that the less you know about this particular party, the better it'll be for you. He doesn't appreciate notoriety."

"Oh, but it's okay for you to know. Fucking mystery man yourself, is that it?"

"I don't get it. Why Toronto? Why not D.C. or the City like always? What could possibly be up here? They start sharin' the wealth?"

"That is the way of it today. Everybody makes a small piece, and nobody sees the big picture, so to speak."

"Makes our job a lot tougher, ya know?"

"I'm certain they didn't have your convenience in

mind when they set it up. Besides, it just means we can charge more for our services."

"Fantastic."

"Just what I wanted to hear. All right, then. Guess we're going back to Ultimate Diecasting."

Inspection Report

Martin sat at his desk and turned on his computer. The mystical alignment of the office supplies had been disturbed by the cleaning staff, so he moved the stapler back into its place as anchor to the holy trinity of stapler, calculator, pen holder. He tore yesterday's page off his daily vocabulary-builder calendar to reveal the word of the day:

Recondite - (reh'kondeit) *a. Secret, hidden, or unknown... removed from ordinary understanding or knowledge, deep or profound.*

"Deep or profound. Merlin's secret scrolls were considered to be quite... recondite. Merlin's recondite scrolls of magic."

"What's that you're mumbling, Marty?"

"Word of the day, Dave."

"Okay, just as long as I know you're not going bug-eyed crazy and muttering and drooling over there."

"Not so far. Check with me after lunch."

"I tell you, Marty. It's just a matter of time for us all." Dave was a 'glass is half empty' kind of guy, who would also take pains to point out that there were smudges all over the glass and a lipstick stain and wasn't this a crack in the side and where did they get this water, anyway, a swamp? Dave's hair was lazy, not conforming to any shape or style. A borderline scowl and his curly, wind-scattered bed head look were always complemented with clothes that just skirted the limits of the company dress code: a turtleneck sweater technically is "a shirt with a collar" and hiking boots are not sneakers per se. His expression was one of perpetual disillusionment, as if he were hearing the last part of a carney's sales pitch and was itching to walk away.

The day's quotes lay stacked in his IN box and Martin surveyed them thoughtfully, making a few notes, setting a few aside to decline, and then putting the rest in a pile for the underwriting checks.

He read his e-mail, which was just the usual internal memos and broker correspondence and a joke about two sailors and a pissing contest. He pulled a folder down from his pile of renewals and set to it. Had a second coffee and began to come to life. Quoted a few, took a few phone calls, did the suck-up thing with the brokers. The majority of the insurance business in Canada was written through brokers and many companies wrote their business exclusively through them. It was like having a sales force that was entirely independent and could choose to sell any customer on your particular coverage or go to any of your competitors instead. Keeping brokers happy was a daily challenge.

Dave came around the corner of Martin's cube just before lunch. "Unbelievable. I just told George

Simpson that I wasn't renewing that shit hole of a repair garage, and he said he'd 'pull the whole goddamn book' if we didn't do it."

"No way!" said Darlene, coming around from the other side of Martin's cubicle.

"Oh, yeah. Second time in a month he's threatened me with that shit. Well, you know Gerry's going to approve it now. And the whole place is going to burn to the ground tomorrow, I guarantee it."

"Why don't we call his bluff?" said Martin. "He'll just keep pulling that trick until we do."

Dave shook his head sadly. "No, no, Martin. Now you know this is a growth year, and head office is on us to write more business, not chase it away."

"There must be something in the water out there in broker-land. I just had a producer ask me if it was okay to put an airport on 'some kind of package,'" said Darlene. "Hello? Is anybody home?"

"At least that's just stupidity and not some fucking broker power play making us do something for the wrong reason," said Dave. His scowl was working overtime.

"I don't know sometimes," said Darlene, crossing her arms and pulling the material tight across her chest, which caused the material in Martin's pants to pull tight across his crotch. He picked up his file folder and opened it across his lap as he pretended to listen to what Darlene was saying while concentrating on not looking at her breasts. "Okay, the vast majority of brokers we deal with are honest, professional, and a pleasure to work with, but there's always a few sleazoids."

Darlene was very attractive. She had raven black hair with big boobs and she was taller than Martin with a lot of confidence and sass. Tells it like it is. Shooting the shit with her like this, in easy camaraderie, he was made acutely aware of his single guy status. This gave him a feeling like indigestion that was way down low in his stomach. It was an ache of some kind. The idea of converting this friendly interaction with a woman into something deeper was right there in front of him every day. It seemed so easy at times, but he knew how complicated it became. And she had a boyfriend, anyway.

"This is the kind of day which reminds us that Franz Kafka was a commercial underwriter," offered Martin. "All hail the patron saint of Underwriting!"

"Sure, Martin," said Dave. "Whatever."

Darlene laughed and returned to her desk.

Martin often marveled at the Kafkaesque qualities to his job. The people who needed their product the most, people with a high exposure to loss by fire, theft, or liability, were the ones they did not want to sell it to. His job was to prevent these kinds of people from buying the product, and trying only to sell it to people who didn't need it as much, people with a low exposure to loss. He often thought of Kafka, the perpetual insomniac, madly scribbling long into the night, imagining himself as a huge bug, a man on trial, a prisoner in a penal colony. What more proof of the pressures of the job was needed? You just had to read the stories to know how he felt, and Martin did both.

Martin noticed a thick fax had come in from the Loss Control Department at Head Office. Ultimate Diecasting, the cover reported. That was fast. Less than a week and here it was. Good to see that "RUSH!" actually corresponded to a notion for these people that they should hurry. He flipped to the back to look at the picture: a pretty standard non-combustible industrial plaza. He checked the protection, and confirmed that it had a monitored alarm system, steel bars on the doors and windows and they had sprinklers. No obvious deficiencies that he could see. Yet.

The narrative section was less clear cut. It described a standard machine shop set-up, with CNC machines for cutting patterns described by a computer, lathes, drill-presses, and a quality control department. Fair enough, but what were they making? The description of products was vague, something about flange rings and some metal casings with an "industrial" application. Application to what? The rep noted in the file that the insured was "cagey" about products and "intensely private" about their customers. U.S. Sales: 75%. Customer(s): confidential. Reading between the lines, Martin could tell he wasn't getting the whole story.

He phoned over to head office to speak to the rep.

"Hi, Walt. It's Martin Porchnik over at Metro. I got your report on Ultimate Diecasting. Thanks for the quick response."

"No problem. I was out that way on another call yesterday, and I dropped by without an appointment. You get a better picture of the normal day-to-day stuff if you don't give them a chance to clean up."

"Sounds like they weren't very forthcoming with information."

"Are you kidding? Just call me a dentist."

Martin laughed because it was expected. "It says here his U.S. customers are 'confidential'. He didn't give you any further explanation of that?"

"No, he showed me the door at that point. I was practically thrown out of the joint, so I got the picture that they were pretty touchy about their customers. You could order an audit of the books if you wanted. It's your right under the statutory conditions, which I sure don't want to be the one to tell him."

"The premium on this thing is only $5000. Gerry would never approve it."

"Well, that's all you're going to get, then. I'm telling you, Marty, it's like water from a stone."

"Okay, thanks, Walt."

He allowed himself a kind of humph noise of frustration as he hung up the phone. Only one more option. He took it in to Gerry.

"Here's that machine shop that Jed Johansen sent in," he said without preamble, barely knocking on her door frame. "The one with the new loss."

She looked up. "Oh, yeah. That was fast. Let's have a look." He handed her the report and sat in the chair opposite her desk. She skimmed the report, nodded at the blurry, faxed photographs, and looked up at him. "Looks fine. So, it was bad luck. Not worth worrying about it."

"I'm still worried. They're not telling us what they're making there. We have virtually no information about products liability. We don't know what they make, and we don't know who their customers are. Walt told me he was practically thrown out of there when he pushed him about his customers."

"So send a note to the broker. I'm sure it's something boring, just like it sounds. 'Flange rings and casings.' Don't worry so much."

"You pay me to worry."

"Oh, yeah. Well, go and do it somewhere else. Kidding! But really, if you could."

Back to the cube. He was already composing the memo in his mind. *"Please confirm the following: Who are the insured's major clients? For what end products does the insured produce parts? Who provides the designs for these parts and who checks them prior to use?"* He could also see himself waiting until quarter past hell freezing over to hear from the broker. This was a Johansen, after all. Oh well, he sighed. He'd just have to push a little.

"Earth to Martin."

"What?" he said. "Oh, George. What the hell, bro? You're early."

"Making good time today, I guess. Did you need more time to stare off into space?"

Martin laughed. "No, it's fine. Come with me

while I package it up."

George waited while Martin packaged up the head office mail, joking and talking the whole time. When it was ready, they again agreed that they'd have to get a drink after work some day and George was out the door. Martin wondered if they'd ever get that drink or whether it was just the kind of pleasantries people exchanged out of habit.

He returned to the puzzle that was the main file on his desk, his own personal detective mystery to be solved.

The Opportunity

After the morning deliveries were completed,
George's lunch was a vendor veggie dog in Nathan
Phillips Square, looking up at the space ship which
had landed there in 1965. That is what the building
looked like. It was a circular edifice covered by a
shallow white dome and flanked by twin curved
office towers and the whole thing sat on a raised
section of square concrete which looked like a
landing pad. It was designed by an architect from
Finland who won the international architecture
contest launched by Toronto's then mayor.

Since that time, City Hall had been run by aliens;
whether worse or better than by the humans
previously, no one could decide. Some day, people
said, the saucer would rise up into the sky fully
loaded, and return to the planet Politicia.

The regular crowd of seagulls crowded around
George's concrete flower-box seat. "How 'bout a little
of the bun, guv'nor?" "Just a few crumbs for a
starving gull." "Make sure it hasn't touched the hot
sauce—I've been burned before." "Don't worry about
these guys, I can take 'em." "Hey, offa me, Beak

Boy!" "You want a piece of me?" "I'm gonna pluck you clean, Butterball!"

Two gulls chased each other across the sidewalk, both madly flapping wings, and going "Aaiiik! Aaiik! Aieek!" George tossed the crowd a piece of his bun, torn up into small pieces. There was a mad skirmish for share of the bounty.

"There, that's all you're getting. You guys are getting fat. What a morning, lads! Beautiful day for riding, nothing but light parcels today. Man, what a great job this is! What other job would let me dress like this, work outdoors, feel the wind in my hair?"

He was only half-way through his meal and so far sans mustard spills, when a bike skidded to a stop in front of him.

"Yo, G.G.," said Chet. He was wearing his black helmet with the skull and cross bones, khaki green shorts with a million pockets and a Pokemon t-shirt. His eyes were hiding behind sunglasses, just like all the couriers, but even just the scabby, scarred look of his lips and nose and the dull, open-mouthed smile showed up his lack of intellectual prowess, George figured. "What's up, my man?"

"My rent," said George.

"I heard that. Whatcha doin' here?"

"Not much. Just chillin' with the gulls."

"And havin' a little lunch."

"Yep. You eaten?"

"Oh, yeah. I get hungry real early, man."

They both nodded and Chet leaned on the front of his handlebars. He finally got to the point.

"So, listen, man. Me and some of the other guys have been pullin' a few extra deliveries on the side for extra dough, and I was wondering if you'd be down with summa that."

"Sure, I can always use more work for the slow periods. This isn't off the dispatcher?"

"No, this is a, whaddayacallit, private party. We get a package and an address along with a hundred cash, no questions asked."

"A hundred cash? Sounds like you guys are running drugs, Chet."

"I don't ask no questions, man. It's just a package to me, you know. It could be anything. I take the money, I make the drop. Simple."

"It doesn't sound simple to me. Sounds like 5-10 years, possession with the intent to traffic in narcotics."

"Yeah, well, I just thought you should know. The extra bread is really nice, man. Think about it, why don'tcha?"

George said nothing.

"Yeah, well, are you going to the bar tonight?"

"Of course."

"Okay, then. See you there?"

"Yeah."

"Take it easy, G.G."

He held out his fist, and George gave him a bump. "See you, Chet," he said, as Chet pedaled away slowly.

Chet looked back at him over his shoulder. "You know it." He looked away just as he was about to collide with an old man in a three piece suit, swerved and sped away towards downtown.

George found himself unable to finish his veggie dog, so he treated the gulls to a rare feast, and broke up the last half into tiny pieces and distributed it amongst the crowd. "Yeah, this is a great job, guys. Nothing but opportunities."

He brushed off his hands, had a few gulps of his water, and then got on his bike, coasting down to Queen Street aimlessly. The afternoon pickups were a half-hour away yet and the radio was quiet, so he slowly pedaled around the streets of downtown. Cruised along Queens West over to Bathurst. Up all the way to College.

It was no big thing. It was their problem, not his. Nothing to do with him. He'd just do his job, get paid like always, and go home. What had changed for him? It was the same job it was yesterday. Except idiots like Chet were now making more money than he was. But he was okay with that. He wasn't in it for the money, as he had said to Gina many a time.

And what if he did? Would it really be wrong? Like Chet said, you didn't really know what was in the package, so how can it be immoral? The extra money would really be nice, and it would show Gina that the job could be worthwhile. Not that he had to do that. But how could he explain the extra money? It would look pretty suspicious. Maybe he'd just bank it all for a rainy day, and surprise her. Who the hell was he kidding?

Coasting along College, past Spadina, he suddenly

found himself in front of number 230, the Faculty of Architecture. So many hours, so many projects, essays, arguments over formal classicism and suchlike. Everything was so clear cut, yet so intense. He rode along in front of the university bookstore, and decided, what the hell, take a little tour through campus.

Turning down St. George, the first thing he passed was the Faculty of Engineering building, which he absolutely hated. Its institutional warehouse facade was so bland, so efficient and merely utilitarian, lacking any kind of imagination or sense of design—the same thing he thought about engineers themselves. He cut through the alleyway to University College, one of his favorite buildings.

It was the centerpiece of the entire campus, an adaptation of the Romanesque Style by F.W. Cumberland in the 1850's. The first non-denominational college in Canada, and the model for the aspirations of universities everywhere today. A thing of history, of beauty preserved. The summer students were wandering unhurriedly around the paths, relaxing on steps, soaking up the sun. No worries of any kind. And they didn't know how lucky they were to be here. He hadn't. He'd taken it all for granted. Was eager to get out into the real world and start architecting. Should have savored the sun.

Glancing at his watch, he suddenly noticed that he was late for his first pickup. Cursing himself, he quickly accelerated across the campus and over to

College Street, across to University Avenue, and then flew downtown.

"You're late," said the receptionist, holding out the envelope and receipt in her supercilious way. She loved this, as he was usually waiting for her.

"Bite me, slag-bitch," he would have said if his internal monologue had been projected onto his larynx at that exact moment. "Sorry, traffic," he said lamely, out loud. He tore off her copy and stalked out the door. He put on his Ray-Bans outside the door and took a deep breath. Lots of time to get back on schedule.

By the time he hit his last stop, he was a half-hour behind, and the slag-bitches were waiting for him behind every door. All except Janice, who was pleasant as always: "Running a bit behind, eh, George? Don't worry about it. It's usually us who keep you waiting. Have a good day, now."

When it was all done, he thought about going to the bar, but for once, this was not a pleasant thought. All those smug bastards with their hundreds in cash and their no questions asked. Laughing behind their hands at him. Idiot, doesn't know a good opportunity when he sees it. What else? Pompous ass, won't drink with the rest of us, so superior, vegetarian, thinks he's better than us, won't take the same money we do, obviously thinks we're lowly scum.

He couldn't face them, couldn't offer the nightly toast to Hermes that he had made up; all that crap would be seen in a new light, now. He had to get home, but his legs felt like jello. He usually used the break at the bar to refuel and get his strength back for the long ride home.

Feeling a combination of shame and a strange queasiness he hadn't been able to shake since lunchtime, he carried his bike down the steps of the King Street subway station. He put his token in the gate and lifted his bike over the rail.

"Hey, you can't bring that on the train in rush hour," yelled the ticket booth operator.

"Bite me, slag-bitch," he finally said. He walked onto the train just as the doors were closing.

By the time he climbed the stairs to their apartment and locked up his bike on the fire escape, he could barely haul his creaking carcass over to the couch to crash. It would be a couple of hours till Gina got home, and he wasn't particularly hungry. He lay still and stared at the ceiling, his stomach still in knots.

The Contact

Mr. Smith was reading a book when his cell phone rang. He put the book down on his bedside table and answered on the second ring. "Hello?"

"---"

He sat up on the bed and picked up a pen just in case. "Yes, I am going by 'Smith,' again. I find it amusing."

"---"

"The usual two," he said, wincing in anticipation.

"---"

"I know. It was unavoidable. They do possess the requisite skills."

"---"

"That won't be a problem."

"---"

He stood up and walked over to look out the window. "No, they can't keep the plans on a computer. It's too easy for information to be passed on or stolen electronically. They exist only in blueprint form."

"---"

"We have an inside contact who has given us the

necessary information. They will go in tomorrow night after we contact our source."

"---"

"Yes, the usual fee."

"---"

"The situation is secure."

"---"

"This will be their last operation. Once the task has been completed, I will be dealing with them myself." His eyes flicked over to his briefcase as if to reassure himself it was still there.

"---"

"I'll be on the plane with the package by the end of the week."

Mr. Smith pressed the "End" button.

The Fight

George sat on the couch. He hadn't yet had a shower and he was sweaty, tired, and dirty. Spread out around him were his old university textbooks, which he was flipping through absent-mindedly. Remembering all the theorems, diagrams, structural stratagems, design styles, columnar motifs and line and space complements that he had had to draw and memorize and delineate in the multi-thousand word essays. At the time, it had all seemed worthwhile, was a dream come true. Something he'd planned since he was in tenth grade art class with Mrs. Dewicki. Now what did he have to show for it? Fuck all.

And now the job that he at least enjoyed, even if it wasn't going anywhere, thank-you Gina, was going to hell because of that dumb ass Chet and his drug-running cronies. These were people he used to call his friends. He thought he knew them, but obviously he had misjudged them and the seeming simplicity of the job. So what was he left with? Fuck all. A job he couldn't get, a job he could no longer do, and nothing else he really wanted.

He couldn't take their offer. Running drugs was stupid. There's a reason they call it being a mule. Intelligent people know that petty crime doesn't pay. Someone down the line will tell the wrong person, who tells two friends, and so on. Eventually he'd find himself handing his no-questions-asked-package to a friendly narcotics officer. Who had a few questions for him. Not to mention that it was immoral. Being a moral person was such a burden sometimes.

He couldn't work with these people anymore. He knew what was going on. To remain silent made him a possible accomplice, or even worse… a liability to their little scheme. There were clearly darker forces behind all this, who wouldn't be as easy-going as his courier buddies. Someone might not like the idea of him knowing what he knew and not going along. Someone who might show up with a package of tasty lead just for him in a dark alley some night.

But the idea of looking for another job was actually frightening. Starting from the bottom, taking a "responsible" job with future prospects was a whole lifestyle choice that he had been putting off. The easy-come, easy-go lifestyle of a bicycle courier was very simple. It had become a safe place where he had an excuse for not being a success. *The whole architecture thing didn't work out, so now I'm stuck in this cool, go-nowhere job, poor me, lucky me.*

It was an identity. And change was scary.

"Hi, Georgey," called Gina from the kitchen. "Sorry I'm late. Have you eaten?"

"No," he said without getting up.

"Oh, good. Let's go out. I can't face making any...
what's wrong with you?"

He looked up from the couch. "Nothing."

"You haven't showered, and you have all your
architecture books out. Bad day?"

"Not particularly. Just tired. You know, hump day.
Busy."

"Okay, well go clean up and we'll go out and then
have an early night. I'll be on top tonight and you
won't have to do any work."

"Sounds good to me." He smiled and kissed her
lips as she sat on the couch next to him.

"I'm pretty beat myself."

He had a quick shower and changed and bounced
back a bit. They went to an Italian place a block away
and had the special, Eggplant Primavera. Flat bread
and hummus to start and two Pellegrinos on ice.
They chatted for a while about Gina's day and
something her Mom had called her about that was
happening on Sunday. It was a relief to focus on
something else, but he could feel her looking at him
and knowing something wasn't right.

"So how was this day of yours, if not so bad?" she
said after their entrées arrived.

"Same as usual. Ride around a lot of different
places. Pick up. Drop off. You know the routine."

"Nothing out of the ordinary?"

"No, not really. Oh, yeah. Well, there was one
thing. I was talking to Chet today, and you won't
believe what that idiot is doing."

She leaned forward. "Oh, do tell. I love Chet

stories."

"He's doing extra deliveries on the side. 'No questions asked' for a hundred cash each time."

"So we're obviously talking about drugs. Are any of the other guys doing it? I can't see him coming up with this on his own."

"Yeah, a lot of them, apparently."

"And he offered this to you."

"Yeah."

"I know you said no."

"Of course. I'm not stupid."

"Those idiots," she said, shaking her head. "They're going to get caught. The more people they tell, the more likely it is that someone will eventually snitch to the cops, and the whole ring will end up getting busted."

George chewed his food and nodded.

"So what are you going to do?"

"Nothing."

She gave him a look.

"What?"

"What do you mean, what?" she said.

"What's that look for?"

"Tell me you're not thinking about staying on there."

"Of course I am. What's wrong with that?"

"You have to get out. Now."

"No, I don't."

"You can't keep working with them, knowing what you know. Even if they are stupid about this, the people they are dealing with are not, and they won't like it that you know about their operation and refused to go along."

"What would they care? I said no. What are they going to do?"

"Hurt you, try to scare you, who knows? You could end up getting killed."

"Don't be so dramatic. I told Chet I didn't want any part of it, and he was totally cool with it."

"Who cares what Chet thinks? You think he's in charge of this?"

"No, but maybe he didn't tell anyone that he told me."

Gina put down her fork with a loud clack. "Who do you think he's recruiting for? You think Big Eddy isn't in on this? You've got to quit. Like tomorrow. You can get a job anywhere for the same money you're making. It's over."

"I'll be the one to say when it's over," said George, angry now and not trying to hide it. "And I say it's fine."

"The fuck it is. Are you really going to be this stupid?"

"What's stupid is quitting a job because of something my co-workers do. It has nothing to do with me."

Gina pushed her chair back and threw her napkin onto her plate. "That's fine. I'll come and identify the body. Enjoy your dinner." And she stalked out of the restaurant.

George sat at the table for what seemed like a long time. He tried to finish his dinner, but it was doing a great job of sticking in his throat. He paid the bill and walked home the long way, around the neighborhood, looking up at the dark, limitless sky. He looked in the lit windows of houses filled with families, people with go-somewhere jobs, kids kicking around in the basement, dog in the backyard whining at the door. Car lease payment due next week, three bedroom mortgage closing in around them while they sleep, mouths open snoring from every room, mouths that had to be fed. A dog came running out from one of the houses, giving him hell all the way.

"Hey, you! Hey, you! Don't come any closer! I'm rough and tough. I'm protecting the rest of the pack, who are inside sitting around the noisy box."

George paused to wait for his arrival. "Hey, buddy. It's okay, I'll just stay out here on the sidewalk. I'm not comin' in there."

"That's good, then. You smell okay to me. Mmm, very good. What's that on your hand? Eggplant with tomato sauce? That's real garlic in there. Not too spicy. It's good, but I prefer the veal, myself."

"Um, make yourself at home. Don't be shy about drooling on me."

"Tasty. Oh, oh, yeah, that's right. Right behind the ear there. Harder would be good. Oh, yeah, liking that."

George withdrew his hand from over the fence. "Well, I gotta go, guy. I'm going to need to wash these hands. No offense. Take it easy."

The dog sat down with his nose still poking

through the fence and watched him as he walked away. "Bye, tasty guy. You're all right."

When he got back home, the couch was piled with blankets with his pillow on top and the bedroom door closed. When he woke up the next morning, Gina was already gone. He felt like shit.

He called her at work, but got her voice mail. He hung up without leaving a message. Fucked if he was going to grovel to her when she was the one who had over-reacted. The idea that he was in some kind of danger just because he didn't accept a business offer from a colleague. And what did he really know, anyway? Whole lotta nothin'. Hundred bucks. Extra package once in a while. Just not for him.

He got ready and hit the road, really pushing himself, passing cars like they were standing still, which of course they sometimes were. He braked outside of the Midtown Cafe at just a bit after 8:30, lock on, seat off and helmet under his arm. Coffee was burning his tongue inside of two minutes as he checked the paper. The radio crackled on his hip. Early. "Yo, G.G. What's up? Over."

"Your cholesterol count, over."

"Funny. Big Eddy says he wants to see you at the bar tonight. Over."

George paused. That was the last thing he needed. "Um… tell him I can't make it today. I'll see him tomorrow. Over."

"Ten-four, good buddy. I always wanted to say that. I've got a pickup at 280 King Street, number 801. You finished your coffee?"

"I am now. I'm on it."

He left his coffee to get cold, and gently set a two dollar coin on the table next to the saucer.

Martin Gets an Offer

Martin could not believe his eyes when he saw his file appear on the Large Loss listing from head office. How on earth did a small break-in get to be over a hundred grand? But there it was: *Ultimate Diecasting - $120,000 reserve.* This thing was a nightmare from the start and now he had to complete a Large Loss report for the higher-ups that they would all be scrutinizing and talking about. He didn't really want it associated with him at all, let alone have it define the quality of his underwriting. This policy file wouldn't stand up to much scrutiny. He barely had it entered on the system and now this.

Thinking about the circumstances of the loss got him going in circles all over again. What weren't they getting here? Something was missing or he would understand it better. He didn't like not understanding risk; it made him feel out of control. There wasn't enough premium in the world for a risk that couldn't be quantified and, preferably, rated per hundred dollars of coverage.

The way underwriters understand risk is based on history, by class of business. So for every machine shop there had ever been across Canada, the *Insurers Advisory Organization* kept track of every claims dollar that was spent on fires, break-ins, windstorm and water damage, etc., for the whole group. Then this amount was compared against the entire amount of property coverage at risk and a rate is developed per hundred of coverage. Where underwriting comes in is in applying critical judgment to decide what credits or surcharges should apply to the base IAO rate considering factors that bring the risk closer to the best of class or make it worse. Not knowing all the factors kept an underwriter awake at night. Which meant that it was time for more coffee.

Pouring himself a cup and reading the list of postings and health and safety bulletins, chatting with Janice and then sauntering back to his desk, checking voice mail and taking note of who wanted a piece of him. The crisp new file was still open on his desk. On the surface, it appeared to be a good risk. All the security and protection was there. But something strange happened when thieves broke in and didn't steal the things that had the most obvious value, which meant there was something of value they were looking for that Martin didn't know about. He tried staring off into space for awhile to see if it would come to him.

"Hey, Martin. It's me, Reality. I'm calling you. Hello?"

Martin snapped out of it and saw that George was leaning against the wall of his cubicle. Thank God, a diversion.

"George, my friend, how are you?" said Martin, standing.

"I'm all right. How about you?"

"I'm three coffees over my quota and it hasn't helped."

"Sorry to hear that. I think packing a courier envelope is exactly the therapy you need."

"When isn't it?" Martin said as he started towards the mail room. George fell in step beside him. "We have a ship's anchor that needs to go to the Port Credit marina. You up for it?"

"Sure, if you can afford it. Strap it on me, pay me the eight thousand bucks and I'll be on my way."

Martin laughed and grabbed the entire pile of mail, jamming it all in the envelope. He pulled the adhesive strip off the envelope, sealing the mad jumble of paper inside. He didn't even bother to sort it by department. Didn't feel like it. Felt like nothing more than a cold beer sliding down his throat right about now. He handed the envelope to George, who stowed it inside his satchel.

"Hey, how about that drink tonight?" said Martin. "You up for it?"

"Um. Yeah. Why not? I could really use one."

They walked to the front door, George putting on his sunglasses.

"Great," said Martin. He could taste the beer already. "Where do you want to meet?"

"Someplace casual. I'm not exactly dressed in my executive grubs today."

"How about East Side Mario's over on Front

Street?"

"That'll work. Say, 6 o'clock?"

"I'll be there," said Martin. He waved as George passed through the double doors on the way out. He walked back in the direction of his desk trying to settle on something he could do between then and 5 o'clock that didn't have anything to do with Ultimate Diecasting.

The Dinner Idea

George locked up on Front Street in front of the Convention Center. There were always people milling around there, so the bike would be safe. Even so, he took the seat with him just in case. From there, he walked up Front to East Side Mario's, a bar slash restaurant near the end of University Avenue which catered to tourists and people downtown to see the Leafs, Raptors or Blue Jays. Martin was already seated inside with a beer in front of him, so George bypassed the hostess stand and joined him at the table.

"Hey, Martin. So, did your day get any better? Oh, hi. Yeah, can I get a Pellegrino with ice? Thanks."

Martin raised his glass to him. "So, how's the courier business these days?"

"Tough business lately. Gotten very cutthroat."

"Yeah? How so?"

"Um. A lot of new players. Fierce competition."

"I guess it's becoming a pretty big business. I seem to see more of you all the time. And all year round, too."

"Yep."

"What's it like riding the bikes in winter?"

"Winter is just like any other time of the year, except the cars go a little slower and are even more unpredictable. It's not a problem for a bike, though. My tires are better than a car's for snow and ice."

"Wow. Still, I guess it's pretty scary sometimes."

"Just about any day of the year can be scary."

"So, how did you get into that line of work, if you don't mind my asking. Have I asked you that before?"

"I look like I'm too smart to be riding bike for a living? Thanks, I am."

"Nothing wrong with being a courier. I was just curious."

"I know. I love my job. You couldn't chain me to a desk for twice my salary."

"They don't chain us anymore. It's a magnetic constriction collar these days."

"Oh, so that's what keeps those white shirt collars so stiff. What about you? How did you get into insurance?"

"Family. Nobody ever grows up wanting to go into insurance. You either know someone in the business, or you get in by accident, right out of school or something, and you never get out. It's not so bad. I actually kind of like my job most of the time."

"That's not a bad thing. It's important to like what you do."

"Yeah, I get to flex my brain muscles once in awhile. And work with numbers, which I'm good at."

They talked about university for a while, relating stories from their undergrad days. George was feeling fidgety, his mind often drifting away from the conversation. There was a nervous feeling in the pit of his stomach that he couldn't shake. Maybe it was because he was so used to being at the bar at this time every day. Maybe it was hunger.

"Did we have menus at some point?" said George. "I'm kind of hungry. You want to get dinner, since we're here?"

"Um... sure. I could go for that. Where's the guy?"

"I've got to make a phone call. I'll grab some menus on my way back."

George got up and went to the front of the bar near the washrooms and phoned home. Nobody home, or nobody answering? The machine was on, so he left a message. Short and to the point. Just where he was and that he'd be late. Then he found a couple of menus at the hostess station and headed back to the table.

"Here you go. What do we feel like tonight?"

"They usually do a good steak here. New York strip?"

"I do not partake of the flesh of cattle."

"No steak?"

"No cows, or pigs, or beasts of any sort."

"You? A vegetarian?"

"Yep."

"Interesting. I never would have pictured that about you. So what made you give up the meat?"

"You mean, is it a religion thing?"

"I hadn't even thought of that. Usually it's a cruelty thing, I'm guessing."

"I just feel better when I eat this way. Why do you eat meat?"

"Because it tastes so damn good. Nice juicy steak with garlic and mushrooms. Mmm. Tell me you don't miss it sometimes."

"Never. I never really liked meat when I was a kid. I was always a little bit grossed out by it. Only ate the most processed kinds of meat I could find. Nothing off the bone. And then when I did some reading on the subject, and talked to some vegetarians I knew, I was convinced."

"So are you one of the ones who eat cheese and eggs, or are you a vay-gun?"

"I'm mostly vee-gan."

"So you can have cheese?"

"I can have whatever I want. They're my rules. But I mostly stay away from all animal products if I can."

"All this talk about steaks is making me really hungry. Where the hell is the guy?"

"You made the classic mistake of being hungry. Don't you know that hungry people are invisible to waiters? They can only see bitchy people. Hey, buddy! Little help over here? Yes. We've decided to eat. I'll have the 'Angel Hair Primavera' and the salad to start. No cheese, thanks."

"And for you, sir?"

"I'll have the New York strip with the salad as well. And another beer."

"Another Pellegrino, sir?"

"Sure."

"I'll be right back with your bread and salad."

Martin drank off the remains of his beer. "So, is Gina a vegetarian, too?"

"Yeah, she is."

"That must make things easier."

"I guess so."

"How long have you lived together?"

"Since university, which is a fair few years."

"Any talk of marriage?"

"Bite your tongue. What about you, when are you getting married?"

"Married? I'd need a girlfriend first."

"You're not seeing anyone?"

"No, not right now. Not for a long time, really."

"Anything in particular responsible for the dry spell?"

"Or anyone? Yeah, I've had a couple of relationships end badly."

"Nothing ends well. It is either good and keeps working, or it ends. Usually badly."

"I suppose. But everything seemed to be going along so well with Jenny. We were seeing each other all the time..."

Martin went on, but George wasn't following what he was saying. He thought of waking up that morning with Gina gone, and that feeling in the pit of his stomach. His salad wasn't exactly going down easy. She was probably home by now and had got his message. She had probably expected him to come right home so they could talk about it. As if that was a scene he was looking forward to. She only wanted to hear one thing, and he wanted, what? To stall? To agree? He couldn't face it. He needed time to think things through for himself first.

"And so, that's when she said that it was over. I wasn't consulted. We're still 'friends.' We're just the kind of friends who haven't spoken once since that night."

George blinked and tried to pick up the thread of the conversation he had missed. "That's a tough one. But what about getting back up on the bike and all that?"

"Why bother? I have no luck with women. I've seen how it ends, and it's not worth it. Besides, I'm not exactly dating material."

"What's luck got to do with it? It's all about self-esteem, my man. You've got to love yourself before someone else can. And I hear a lot of negativity coming from you."

"Yeah, I guess."

"How are your dinners, gentlemen? Can I get either of you another drink?"

"Great, yeah, another Pellegrino."

"And another beer, sir?"

"No, make it a ginger ale. Diet."

"We have Diet Coke."

"That's fine. Thanks."

George took some bread to dip in the garlicky oil at the bottom of his bowl. "So, anyway. What went wrong with your day? You were saying, back at the office."

"Oh, one of my risks had a loss."

"Hold up. Risks? Loss? What are we talkin' about here?"

"Yeah, sorry, insurance terms. A risk is a policy or insured location and a loss is a claim that we have to pay out money on."

"Don't you guys have to pay claims all the time?"

"Yeah, but this one bothers me. It's been kind of... suspicious. Right from the start. Of course, nobody else sees it that way."

"Suspicious how?"

"First of all, the broker went over my head when I'd already said no to writing it over the phone with little or no information. Then the inspector went out to question the guy about what kind of products they were making and who their customers were, and he was practically thrown out of the place. The guy acted like someone with something to hide. Wouldn't give us any specifics as to what he was making, and said his customer list was confidential."

"So?"

"Well, first of all, insurance is based on the principle of utmost good faith, and that means, among other things, not hiding anything from us."

"So? Lots of guys are paranoid about keeping their customers secret. I've gotten a lot of flak over envelopes that have come open en route, and guys thinking I'm into industrial espionage or something. Trying to steal their customers away somehow."

"Yes, but we are insuring their products' liability. That means that if they are making cribs, and some 6-

month-old baby gets his head stuck in the bars down
in Tempe, Arizona, and the parents sue him for a
million bucks because of the bruises on junior's head,
we answer the lawsuit on his behalf. Pay the lawyers,
pay any costs, pay the judgment against him.
Everything. So we have a right to know what he's
making, and who or what it could hurt."

"Okay, I'm with you. So what did he say he was
making?"

"Flange rings and industrial casings."

"For what?"

"That's just it. We don't know anything. So then,
Sunday night, the place was broken into. And we're
talking professional thieves here, no amateur job.
They cut the line on the alarm system so it wouldn't
go off, and then removed iron bars from the frame, if
you can believe it. But do they take the standard
things? Hand tools or expensive computers? Not
these guys. They went right for the locked file
cabinets and stole nothing except plans, blueprints,
schematics, and design specs."

"All right. Well, you didn't say that. That's
definitely suspicious. So they're making something
for someone else, and these thieves wanted to steal
the design for it?"

"That's about the size of it. So I want to find out
what they're making, and then void the policy for
non-disclosure, which means there was something
essential to our understanding of the risk that they
didn't tell us, which would have made us change our
mind about taking the policy at all, probably. And

under the terms of utmost good faith, we can return their premium money, say the policy was void, and never existed, and not pay the claim."

"Okay, well, that's a pretty big leap to be making, when you don't even know what it is they're making. And whether that would have made you change your mind about it."

"Yes, but how can I know? It's clear to me that this is not a standard machine shop. These flange rings and metal casings are part of something else that someone wants very badly, and I don't think it's piping, plumbing, or ducts."

"I see what you mean."

"And the adjuster was giving me a hard time about it. I didn't even want to write it in the first place. My manager bound it over the phone; I was just putting the file together. That kind of thing bothers me, for some reason. I mean, I know Jason is a blow-hard, and I should just ignore him, but he gets under my skin. Pretty stupid, eh?"

"So where do you go from here?"

"I just wait to see what happens. The claims department takes over from here, and they'll deal directly with the insured."

"You mean you don't even get to investigate this?"

"No, my job is just on the underwriting end. Sort of like sales."

"Well, that's stupid. Who knows the 'risk' better than you? You should be allowed to get involved in these things. Sounds like this Jason guy isn't going to be worth much."

"I've never thought so."

"So why don't we investigate it?"

"What do you mean?"

George looked at his watch. Gina would still be up, and waiting to talk to him. "Let's go out there and check it out."

"Now? Tonight?"

"Why not? I want to see this place for myself. Do you know where it is?"

"Yeah. 50 Silver Star Boulevard. It's an easy name to remember. But we can't just go out there and snoop around."

"Who says we can't?"

"Well, what are we going to be able to see just from looking in the window?"

"It's a start. Maybe they have a night shift."

"No, the inspection report said the hours were 7am to 7pm. 25 employees, in business for 18 years. They run a $250,000 CNC machine 12 hours a day, and have sales of over $5 million."

"Wow, that's some memory."

"It's been bugging me."

"So, let's go out there. Have you got a car?"

"Yeah, but..."

"But what? You got some other plans for tonight?"

"No."

"Well. We can't let these criminals get away with this. They just walked in there, obviously professionals, repeat offenders, and they're still out there, committing crimes. Let's at least take a look around. Maybe we'll see something that will trigger an idea in our minds, and we'll be able to solve this, and put those bastards behind bars. They broke in. To your risk. It's personal, baby."

"Yeah, I guess that's what I've been feeling. It is personal. All right, what the hell. Let's do it."

They motioned for the bill, and finished the last of their dinners. Martin was a bit odd, but really a good guy once you got to know him. He seemed a bit repressed, and in need of someone to expand his horizons. And George felt strangely resentful of these criminals who were at large somewhere, maybe ready to pull another job. Wonder how much they were being paid? Break in, steal some plans, hand them over, no questions asked.

"How far is it to your car?"

"It's up at Yonge and Finch."

"You parked at Yonge and Finch?"

"No, I live there. I take the subway in to work everyday. My car is in the underground parking lot in my building."

"Well, how environmentally-friendly of you."

"It's cheaper than parking."

"Oh, yeah. That, too. So we'll subway it up, and then go from there."

"All right, but we're just going to look around."

"What do you think, that I'm going to break in myself?"

"No," said Martin. "But I just don't want to take any chances. And what about your bike? Won't it be stolen?"

George laughed and shook his head.

Change of Scene

They each paid their bills, Martin worrying about how much he had spent and the impact it would have on his weekly budget. He shouldn't have had that second beer. He could get a six-pack for less than he paid for the two in the restaurant. Daylight robbery.

They walked out to the street, crossing York Street on their way to Union Station. They put their tokens in the box and pushed through the turnstile. Martin wondered if people were looking at them as if they were an odd pair.

He wondered what they would talk about on the long train ride. Hadn't they already used up all their conversation at dinner? He tried to think of other good things to talk about on the way down the escalator, which was operating smoothly. If the escalator wasn't moving, he always took the stairs. The Toronto Transit Commission had an excellent safety record, but 75% of all accidents on escalators occurred while they were stopped, just because people took that first stutter step getting on, he guessed. His company was on the liability file for a couple of years and he had monitored the account.

"Did you know that 75% of all accidents on escalators happen when they aren't moving?" said Martin when they reached the bottom. George said he didn't and Martin explained some of the background, at which he looked faintly interested.

They got on a train after a few minutes of waiting, and took seats perpendicular to each other. Looked around at the various posters and advertisements. A crazy man in a grimy sweater and work pants got on at Wellesley and stood in the middle of the car. He was looking straight up, snapping his fingers high in the air, first one direction, then another, and proclaiming in a loud guttural voice, "Never take it from me, never take it from me. Fuckers! Never take it from me," as if performing some bizarre spell or incantation. Then he lowered his arms and walked away towards the other end of the car, nodding and muttering to himself, "That's right, that's right, that's right..."

George looked at Martin and laughed. "Do you think that's the end of a conversation with a person he met an hour ago, or the beginning of a conversation with someone he hasn't met yet?"

"It's an ongoing conversation with himself," said Martin.

"At least he's got someone to talk to."

"Yeah."

The rattling and squealing of the train wasn't conducive to conversation, so they mostly rode in silence the rest of the way to Finch station. Martin tried to read the subway ads to occupy his mind.

The Risk Inspection

Martin opened the door to his apartment and invited George in.

"Let me just get my coat," said Martin. "Aren't you going to need one, too?"

"Actually, I've got a pair of jeans and a sweatshirt in my satchel. Do you mind if I use your washroom to change?"

"No, go ahead."

"Your place looks incredibly clean, and, um, functional."

"It's small. You can say it. But I don't need a lot of room. It's just me, and it was the most inexpensive one bedroom I could find. So it's worth the trade-off in space."

"Avid reader, eh?" said George, looking at the stacks of books leaning up against the overflowing bookshelves.

"Yeah." If only he'd known he was having company he would've cleaned up the place. When was the last time he'd had company?

"And no television. No pictures or prints on the walls. I guess you're not too much of a visual

76

person."

"I'm not much for television. But I've never really thought about whether or not I'm a visual person. I'm not much of a decorator, that's for sure. In my family, that was always the woman's domain, and I just never found the right woman. So I live in an undecorated world. There are worse fates."

"I suppose there are. Well, I'll just go change."

George was a bit dramatic, with his long hair, pierced features, and tattoos. But he was an okay guy. A bit prone to snap decisions. What did they expect to find in an industrial complex at ten o'clock at night? It was something to do, though, and it always felt good to be hanging out with one of the "cool" guys. He'd never really had friends that were so interesting or colorful. Certainly in high school a guy like George would never have hung out with him. That's why he hated high school.

And he had never told anyone about Jenny since they'd stopped seeing each other. It actually felt good to talk about her. Made it seem less traumatic and dire, less a present pain and more a part of the past. Even though he still thought about her all the time. He'd agonized over the break-up again and again. How could all the good stuff have gone bad so quickly? You don't even see it coming, and then *BAM*. There's no way to protect yourself from it.

And there was the stuff he hadn't told him. About how they'd never had sex. She always said he had to wait till after they were married. But she had had sex with previous boyfriends, he knew. Had she become a cold fish, or was it something about him that was undesirable? *Well, no shit, Sherlock. Take a look at yourself.* Whatever. He was better off on his own. It had been good talking about her, though, and George was a good listener.

It was kind of fun, whatever it was they were doing. Maybe this is what cool people did: embarked on ill-advised escapades in the middle of the night. And he did sort of want to see the risk. He never got to do location inspections and this particular location had been plaguing him since he'd first heard the name.

"You ready to go?" asked George, returning from the bathroom.

"Why not? Do we need to bring anything?"

"Not that I can think of. Maybe a flashlight. Do you have a map, so we'll know how to get out there? I don't know Scarborough that well."

"Yes, of course. *Perly's.* Do we have a plan of any sort, or are we just going to go out there and see what happens?"

"See what happens."

"Okay, let's go."

He locked the door and joined George at the elevator. His car was on the second level of underground parking. George whistled in mock admiration as they walked out to his car.

"Ooh, Toyota. What's this thing got, four cylinders? It must torque like a beast."

"Just get in and spare me the wisecracks. It's great on gas."

"But can you cruise chicks? That's what I'm talkin' about."

"No, I'm sure they wouldn't spit on this car if it was on fire."

"Well, we might need to get you a new car for your general image makeover. And definitely not a beige one."

"I didn't know I was getting an image makeover."

"Oh, yes. If you want to get with the ladies, you're going to have to loosen up a bit. We'll work on it."

"Who said I want to 'get with the ladies?' More trouble than they're worth, if you ask me."

"Everybody wants to get with the ladies, hotshot. Fact of life. How about putting it in 'D' so we can get out of here. We haven't got all night, you know."

"Oh, sure. I just like to let it warm up a little."

George gave him a look, and then shook his head. Martin put the car in 'D,' and drove out of the parking garage and up to Finch Avenue, heading eastbound. George fiddled with the *Perly's* guide, looking for Silver Star Boulevard.

"Ah, here it is. So we'll take Finch eastbound all the way to Midland Ave."

"Okay."

Martin drove in silence for a couple of minutes as George familiarized himself with the map.

"So what about this architecture thing? Have you ever thought of starting up the job hunt again?"

"I tried it a couple of times, but there was nothing. The further you get from graduation the less likely you are to get a job. There's a big hole in my resume, you know? Huge. If I don't have a job in my field by now, they figure there must be something wrong with me. Just bad timing for me, I guess. If only I could have waited out the recession, and then graduated. I could have gone part-time, taken basket-weaving. But I don't think my parents would have appreciated that."

"Wow, that is rough."

"It's not that bad. This isn't a sob story. I've done okay. Money isn't everything, and I like my job. It's a great job."

"I didn't mean to imply that it wasn't."

"I know. Sorry, I'm a little sensitive about it because Gina has been harping on me lately that I should find some new career. Which I suppose I should, eventually. Any openings in the insurance world?"

"There's always postings in the staff room. I could keep my eyes open for you, let you know when something comes up."

"Thanks, that's nice of you. But I was just kidding. I don't know if I'm cut out for that kind of work."

"No one is."

"The next one's Midland. You want to go left on Midland, and Silver Star is your first left. Here we go."

They pulled into the industrial park road, which looked very dark and deserted. All along the street were huge non-combustible Industrial plazas or warehouse-type buildings. There weren't too many cars around, and they drove along slowly looking for number 50. It wasn't until the dead end of the street that they came upon it.

"There it is. Hey, there's a car out back."

"Oh, yeah. Should I turn around?"

"Yeah, turn around and drive back toward the front, but don't turn in. Good. Don't drive too slowly. Oh, yeah. There's flashlights moving around in there."

"What?" Martin hit the brakes.

"Keep driving. Turn left here."

"Oh, my god! We've got to call the police."

"No, they're coming out. Pull in here and kill the lights. Right there, back up in between the two buildings. They've got to come by here to get out. We'll see where they go."

"They were really robbing the place!"

"They didn't seem to be carrying anything from what I could see."

"I knew about the repeat burglar phenomenon, but usually they wait until the stolen items have been replaced by the insurance money, and then hit the same place again. But nothing has been replaced yet, and why would they want the same plans twice?"

"Maybe it's somebody new."

"Could be."

"Here they come. Black Ford Taurus. Turning right onto Midland. Okay, pull out, but don't turn on your lights yet."

"What? Are you crazy?"

"No, let's just follow them and see where they go. This is a public street. What's the worst they can do?"

"Shoot at us. Get my address from my license plate number or just follow us home."

"There they are. They crossed over Finch. Um, they're still heading south on Midland. Pull out now. Don't turn on your lights until you see another car. Okay, now. They're still up there. Just try to keep them in sight."

Martin watched the black car in the distance and gripped the steering wheel tightly. This was insane, this was insane, this was insane... he was just an underwriter. He sent memos and kept good files. This was a job for the police. He should never have gone along with this, he shouldn't be consorting with George at all; the man was obviously some kind of deranged lunatic.

"Hey, Marty. Are you trying to crush that steering wheel?"

"No," he snapped.

"Hey, take it easy. We won't take any chances. But we can't let these bastards get away with it. And we're the only ones who know where they are. Let's just see where they're going. Okay?"

"Okay." He eased up on the wheel.

"They're turning on Progress, don't follow them down there. It's too deserted, they'll see us." He pointed at the map. "Step on it, and turn right on Ellesmere. We can pick them up again at Kennedy. They're obviously trying to see if anyone followed them. Tricky stuff. Give it some gas, Marty, I don't want to lose them."

He continued to white knuckle the steering wheel,

driving at just under 20k over the limit so there would be no points taken off his license if he was caught speeding.

George pointed up ahead and to their right. "There they are, turning right off Kennedy. They'll be right in front of us. Slow down a little, let them get ahead. This is perfect. You're doing great. You're a natural at this!"

"Ha, ha." Martin was feeling sick.

"Where do you think they're going? Will they try to pull another job tonight? Okay, they're turning on Warden. Stay back a bit, I can still see them. Maybe they're going for the 401."

The black Taurus continued on in its unhurried way, seemingly not a worry in the world, and suddenly turned off onto a side road.

"Oh, my god!" said George. "They're going to the Holiday Inn. Are they really this stupid that they led us right to their hotel? This is great!"

"Yeah, great. I'm going to need to throw up soon. Just let me know when you're finished risking our lives."

"C'mon, Marty. These guys are idiots. Pull into the parking lot, near the front. Let's see what they do. There's a spot, just turn off the lights and pretend to look at this map, they're getting out of their car."

They held the map between them, George pointing at something near the middle, and they watched out of the corners of their eyes as the two men made their way past the Toyota and over to the hotel lobby without once looking in their direction, walking straight past the elevators and into the hotel bar at the back. They weren't carrying anything and didn't appear to be in any kind of hurry. George opened his door with a grin.

"C'mon, let's go get a drink."

"Why not? You won't rest until we're both dead. We might as well take care of it now, not draw it out."

"Marty, have you ever heard of the Gordian knot?"

"Yeah. What about it?"

"What you've got here is a Gordian knot. And you've been puzzling over it, looking at it from all angles, trying to figure out how to undo the damn thing. Do you know how they finally undid the knot?"

"No."

"Alexander the Great took his sword and cut it down the middle."

"So what does that mean?"

"Sometimes you've got to just give up trying to figure it out and cut right through. Either way, it comes apart."

"Great. Do you have a sword on you? I'd feel a lot safer, actually."

They walked across the parking lot and into the hotel lobby. They looked in the doorway of the bar, and could see the two men sitting at a table near the bar, ordering drinks.

"This is perfect. I'm going to sit at the bar and see if I can hear what they're saying. You sit on the couch over there. When they come out, just follow them onto the elevator. Pretend to push for your floor, but then say, 'Oh, that's my floor.'"

"Why would I do that?"

"To find out what room they're in."

"Oh."

"Are you with me, Marty? We've got nothing to be worried about."

"What, me worry?"

"They don't know who we are. We have the upper hand here. You've got a face that no one would suspect. They won't even look twice at you."

"Okay."

"Hold the door for them so they get off first, and then just walk slowly and pretend to dig for your room key or something. I'll meet you here in the lobby after you see what room they're in. Everything clear? Good. See you soon."

He couldn't even believe he was here. But he felt strangely calm. Nothing had happened so far, and he did want to find out more. What kind of thieves broke in and took nothing? The more he found out about this case, the less it made any kind of sense. And George seemed quite sure that everything would be fine. He'd just have to keep his hands from shaking when he got on the elevator.

George gave him the thumbs up and entered the bar. Martin sat down on the couch and looked around for something to read. Reading would calm him down. He found a tourist brochure and started reading about the CN Tower. A wonder of modern architecture, once the tallest free-standing structure in the world.

Nervously, he surveyed the lobby, compulsively checking for fire exits and signage, extinguishers, and sprinkler heads. He noted the location of the pay phone, and thought again about phoning the police. But what would he tell them? There are a couple of guys having a drink in a bar, and they didn't steal anything? Was that even illegal? He started to feel like he was in a detective story. Following a couple of suspects, checking out his leads, leaning on a couple of two-bit punks. He wondered what Mike Hammer would do, or Matthew Scudder. Probably something stupid, but brave. It was a gamble, but what the hell, you only live once. Take a swig of liquid courage from your hip flask, and go in with both guns blazing.

He looked at his watch: 11:07. His heart was beating so hard, he could feel it in his neck. He was jacked. Couldn't sleep now if he wanted to. He wouldn't be getting his eight hours tonight.

Three Guys Walk Into a Bar

The bar was small and dimly lit, with cheesy brass decor to make it look like a captain's room on a ship. Life preservers, lobster traps, telescopes, nautical compasses, and sailors' hats and clothes adorned the walls. There were four televisions in various corners and one above the bar. A few tables were occupied, some by couples, a few single men hunched over their drinks or watching the game.

George sat at the bar with his Pellegrino, seemingly mesmerized by the game on TV. The two thieves sat at a table right behind him, both of them half turned to the bar. One was bigger than the other and both looked somehow swollen, their meaty noses, ears and lips looking like they'd been recently smacked. Both had short, dark hair and black leather jackets of different styles. They'd been wearing black gloves when they walked in front of Martin's car. Two beers sat on the table, one in front of each of them.

"Well, that was a waste a time."

"I told him we didn't miss nothin."

"Fuckin' Smitty thinks he knows it all."

"Lucky thing it was easy work. That place is such

an effin cake walk, am I right?"

"Piece a fuckin pie."

"No, it's 'piece a cake,' not 'piece a pie.'"

"No, it's 'easy as pie,' fuckface."

"Yeah, but not 'piece a pie.'"

"Whatever the fuck it is, it was easy."

"Way too easy. If we need a place to stay the night sometime, we can go there."

"Why'd they bother with that shit box system? They'd be better off with a dog. At least the mutt could do some damage. Maybe."

"So what are we gonna do now?"

"Fucked if I know. Maybe we should go have a little conversation with our inside source, who ten to one scammed us."

"Smitty said the new contract was supposed to be in last week. We turned those files upside down. If it was in there, we'd have it. We had all the effin time in the world."

"Maybe Mr. I'm-so-smart Smith would like to come with us next time, instead of sittin' around here with his thumb up his ass. What do we really need him for? Useless as tits on a bull, is what he is. We could go back to pullin; jobs on our own and cut him all the way out."

"Guy kinda creeps me out. Real quiet, but looks like he'd freakin; eat ya for breakfast if he had to. And enjoy it, too."

"Let him try. Ram that accent down his throat."

"So what do we tell him?"

"Tell him it wasn't there. Let him do with it what

he wants. It's not my problem."

"What ya gonna do with your cut, huh? Sounded like a lotta dough this time."

"That's another thing. Where does he get off not tellin' us how much the contract is? Like we're a couple pieces a meat."

"He always pays. And pays big, too. Get to stay in nice hotels like this, not those shitty dives like we used to. It ain't all bad."

"Yeah, it's all right."

"So where you gonna go? Tahiti? Amsterdam?"

"Depends on how much. See how much time off it gets me."

They went on about vacation hot spots for a while, and George tried to concentrate on what they were saying, but it became increasingly difficult. He was getting bored of listening to these idiots, who obviously could go on talking about nothing all night.

It wasn't really the kind of information he was hoping for. But it sounded like they were the same guys who had hit it the first time. And there was something they missed, or couldn't find, and had to go back for. Something that they still didn't have.

"Oh, c'mon," Goon #1 said. "The Knicks got to play some defense. You can't let em bring that weak shit to the hole."

"The Knicks suck this year, man," said Goon #2. "With the money they're spending, they should be winning it all."

"They been god awful ever since Ewing left."

"Tell me about it."

"It's all about the free agents next year."

"Yeah, we'll see."

"When we get paid, I think I'll get me a couple of tickets in the front row. Right next to Spike Lee."

"Yeah, you and Spike. Whatever. Watch out for the Dream Police when you get there."

"Ha-ha. I never laughed so hard. You'll see."

"Oh, miss? Can we get another couple beers over here?"

The waitress brought their drinks as George milked his second Pellegrino, still glued to the game, but wondering how much longer this was going to last.

"Thanks a lot, uh... Kristen. You're kinda cute. What are you doin' after you get off work?"

"My boyfriend is coming to pick me up."

"Tell him he can come, too."

"I don't think so," she said and George saw her walk away with her apron strings swinging side to side in her hurry.

The two men laughed as if this was the funniest thing they'd ever heard. They had a few chugs of their beer and fell mostly silent for awhile and watched the game. George had been watching the same game for almost 45 minutes but had to take a look to find out the score. He nibbled on some beer nuts thoughtfully.

Basically, he still knew nothing. Except how boring these two were to eavesdrop on. Ten minutes later, the game was over, and the men finished their beers.

"Check, miss. Don't worry, we won't bite."

More laughter. They paid their bill and walked out

of the bar towards the lobby. George waited a few seconds, and then walked over to their table to see if they'd left anything behind. He looked at the glasses, which would be covered in fingerprints, but what would he do with them? Take them to a crime lab?

He returned to his seat at the bar and hoped that Martin would be able to find out their room numbers. He had the feeling that these two weren't yet finished in town and that this might be valuable information at some later time. The matchbooks had the hotel phone number on them, so he pocketed one and went back to the beer nuts.

* * *

Over in the corner, by the end of the bar, at a small, dark table, his back to the room with a hat on, unnoticed by anyone, but with a very erect posture, sat the silent, solitary figure of Mr. Smith.

Elevator Embarrassment

Although he had been watching the bar for the two men to emerge for almost an hour, Martin was still startled by their appearance in the doorway. He looked down at his CN Tower pamphlet and let them pass by behind him. They looked so huge and ugly and mean. It was all he could do to lift himself off the couch when he heard the elevator doors open.

He rounded the corner and turned down the hallway to the elevators just as the doors were closing. Panicking, he lunged forward and caught the door just before it closed.

"Hold on. One more. Going up? Hee-hee. Oh, that's my floor." He was babbling like an idiot. Would they kill him just so they wouldn't have to listen to him anymore?

Sweat was pouring down his sides from Martin's armpits, which were suddenly drenched, like someone had turned on a faucet. He hummed nervously to himself. The men stared straight ahead and didn't look at him, just as George said they would. Was he that invisible to people? Did he leave so little impression?

The doors opened, and he forgot to hold them aside. One of the men was now holding the door for Martin instead. He was a wall of black leather and dark eyebrows. His eyes were too close together.

"Go."

"No, you first," Martin gulped.

He made an impatient gesture with his arm and his partner moved in behind Martin. "Get awff."

Martin exited the elevator and hesitated ever so slightly, looking both ways. The hallway seemed about equidistant in both directions, so he turned right because he could see a fire exit sign. Not that he was in any shape to outrun anyone. Walking slowly in what he hoped would appear to be an unpanicky way, he noticed that the two men were following him. He could hear their footfalls behind him and could see their tiny reflections in the doorknobs he was passing.

When you think of your own death, you rarely imagine a Holiday Inn as the setting. The carpet was so perfectly uniform and nicely vacuumed, and the whole place so well cared for and smelling so fresh and clean. But he was resigned to it now. Everybody had to go some time. If only he'd eaten more steaks.

Would they miss him at the office? Would his parents be much bereaved? Probably not. Unless it made it onto the TV: *Police found the bloody corpse of one Martin Porchnik, Underwriter, repeatedly stabbed in a Holiday Inn stairwell early Wednesday. Film at 11:00.* "Oh, wake up, dear. Martin is on the news."

As he rounded the corner, he saw an ice machine

inside a little enclave, and, hallelujah, a snack machine. He immediately stopped and turned in, forcing the men behind him to pull up to avoid him.

"Think I'll get a snack," he said, forcing himself to smile at them.

They both looked at him, said nothing, and kept walking down the hallway. Martin rushed over to the snack machine, his hand shaking, looking for change. He pushed some coins into the machine, pressed H-6 and hungrily tore the wrapper off a Mars bar, taking a big bite. The choco-sugary flavor filled his senses, and he closed his eyes, savoring it as if it were life itself. He shook his head and forced himself to walk back out into the hallway. Six or seven doors down, there was a doorway swinging closed.

Munching his chocolate bar and walking along quite jauntily, he passed by the door he had just seen closing, using the barest minimum of his peripheral vision in case someone was looking out the peephole. Weren't those peepholes supposed to protect innocent people from criminals, and not the other way around? He walked to the end of the hallway, and opened the stairwell door and then quickly pushed it closed behind him, sitting down with a huge sigh of relief to finish his chocolate bar. The sugar rush was entirely welcome.

Seven-twenty-five. He could still see the door handle in his mind. When he was finished, he pocketed the wrapper and walked back along the hallway in the direction of the elevators. He had come this far unscathed, so he figured he must be charmed. Reaching the hall where his brief ordeal had begun, he pressed the down button, and the doors opened almost immediately. He took one last look down the hallway, and stepped onto the elevator, almost colliding with someone getting off.

"Pardon me," said a quiet, confident voice with a trace of a British accent.

"I'm sorry," said Martin. "I should look where I'm going."

The man held the door a second and looked Martin over. Martin felt scrutinized and hoped he didn't have chocolate on his face. The man was impeccably attired in a gray pinstripe suit, dark hat, conservative navy tie, and a matching puff in his pocket. "Isn't a bit late to be going out?" he asked.

"Oh, uh... " stumbled Martin. "Just going down for a beer."

"I see," said the man. "Good evening."

The elevator doors closed between them, Martin descending towards the lobby and Mr. Smith walking off in the direction Martin had come.

The doors opened in the lobby and he got off, seeing George sitting in the lobby on the couch. He walked over to him triumphantly.

"Marty! You made it back alive," George said in a quiet voice.

"Mostly."

"Did you get their room number?"

"Yep!"

"Fantastic! Good work, Detective. Fist Bump!"

Martin bumped his knuckles against George's

outstretched fist. The desk clerk looked over in mild annoyance, so Martin sat in the chair next to the couch, motioning for George to sit.

"So what do we do now?" said Martin.

"I don't know. What do you think?"

"What did you find out?"

"Not a lot. They didn't steal anything, like we thought. They report to someone named Mr. Smith and they are the same guys who broke in before."

"Why'd they go back, then?"

"They seem to have forgotten something, or missed something. There was supposed to be some new contract in last week that wasn't there when they broke in the first time. The Mr. Smith guy was apparently angry about this and sent them back. I'm not really sure about that."

"Anything else?"

"Yeah, they kept referring to a contact who gave them wrong information."

"Of course! It had to be an inside job. How else would they have known so precisely what to look for?"

"Another thing was, they were talking about some big money. Going on vacations, season tickets to the Knicks. These guys were pretty boring to listen to, but they were excited about the payoff."

"What could have such a big payoff? The reserve on our file is only a hundred and fifty grand. This thing still doesn't add up."

"Tell me about it."

"So should we call the cops? Tell them what room

they're in?"

"And tell them what? That we were snooping around and saw them not steal anything. The cops would be just as likely to charge us as them. We need to get more on these guys and hand them off to the cops gift-wrapped and ready for handcuffs."

"That's what I was thinking. Well, let's call it a night, and talk more about it tomorrow."

"Good idea. I am bushed, and I still have to ride home from downtown." George reached into his pocket. "Here. I got a pack of matches with the hotel phone number on it. We're probably going to need it."

Facing the Music

He rode the Rocket in from the 'burbs. Although he'd been able to put them out of his mind for a few hours, his problems with Chet and Big Eddy and the other couriers resurfaced once he was alone on the train heading downtown. The decision he knew he had to make was the one that he most didn't want to consider. So he felt stuck in limbo. Talking to Gina only made it worse, because he knew she was right, but couldn't bring himself to admit it, because that would be it for being a courier. It would be over.

But he had to talk to her eventually. He couldn't keep avoiding her like this. It wasn't fair to her. He had called her from the hotel while waiting for Marty, but that was only to check in and let her know he'd be home soon. Stepping off at Union Station, he leaped up the steps three at a time and then quickly down Front to retrieve his bike. Getting his second wind after the earlier adrenaline rush, he booted it home and was there in less than half an hour. The light was still on in the bedroom.

"Hi, honey," he called from the door after locking up outside. He opened the bedroom door and spoke more softly. "Sorry I'm so late. I had no idea it would take this long."

"Uh-huh. It would have been nice if you could've mentioned on your message that you'd be going out afterward."

"I didn't know until we finished dinner."

"That's fine. This is not about you going out with your friend. We had some unfinished business from last night, and I expected you would have wanted to come right home to talk to me."

"I did, but I couldn't talk about it yet."

"Oh, and you can, now?"

"I've thought about what you said, and I can see you've got a point. You voiced all the fears that had been in my head, but I didn't want to admit it. Admitting that meant so many other things that I just couldn't face right then. It took time to sink in, but I'm going to quit. You're just going to have to let me take care of it in my own time. And trust me."

"I do trust you. I just don't know if you know these guys like you think you do. Everything has changed. Don't let your guard down just because you think someone's your friend."

"Don't worry. I won't. I haven't been to the bar in the last two nights. And I probably won't go back there. I just haven't worked it all out in my mind yet. But I'm taking tomorrow to give myself time to think."

"They're going to know something is wrong if you keep on avoiding them."

"I don't care. Let 'em wonder."

99

"Good enough. Come here and hug me, now. I was so worried about you all day."

"No need, see? Your man's still in one piece."

"Baby, I love you."

"I love you, too."

They made love then in that gentle way they did after having had a fight or being apart for a while. Luxuriating in each other's skin, holding each other so close their whole bodies seemed to touch. Just needing that reassuring touch, the physical presence of the lover, and feeling the immediacy of each other's need. After, they held each other softly and quietly in the dark, neither wanting to break the spell.

Now what?

The mirror didn't lie: the follicles at the front were sparse. They got thicker further back, but how long till the clearcut spread across the land, and he was entirely deforested? Martin looked at his hair, which was just kind of swooped over and parted on the left. No comb-over, just side part and left long all around. No chemicals or goop in his hair, so it looked a bit "mad-scientistish" when it got all messy in the wind or something. He really did need a haircut. And a new barber. One who didn't go by such an antiquated moniker.

He got dressed, leaving the tie until after breakfast, and checked the fridge for food: milk for his cereal, a few condiments, ham, swiss cheese, butter, OJ. Not much in the way of salad fixins or fruit. That can't be healthy. He made a mental note to investigate the produce aisle on his next grocery shop.

He poured out a bowl of Fruit Loops and milk, reached for the sugar, but decided against it. Munching contentedly, he wondered what healthy people ate for breakfast. The box said he was getting 11 essential vitamins and minerals, but somehow he felt it couldn't be this easy. The unlikely rainbow coloring on the toucan's beak in the box illustration didn't help to reassure him about the overall quality of the product.

Breakfast finished, he looped his neck with silk, tightened the hangman's knot and stood in front of his mirror for an appraisal of the full package. Portly, with rumpled attire that didn't fit quite right (but had been great value, bought during an end of season sale), receding mad scientist hair... what a catch! Single women look out, here he comes in his beige Tercel. Vroom, vroom, it whispers. Women say, "What was that?" "Did you hear something?"

The Finch Rocket station was unexpectedly busy, due to some delay, so he had to stand up on the subway train to downtown. Luckily, he got a pole, because he simply couldn't do the kind of free-standing train surf that hardcore commuters seemed to master. He didn't have the balance for it.

They rolled into Union Station at a quarter past eight. He allowed himself to be swept along by the crowd to his destination, and rode the elevator for 46 floors with the urge to fart, butt cheeks silently clenched until he got off and sought the relief of a discreet chuff in the men's washroom while he checked his hair. Entered the office at 8:30 on the dot.

"Good morning, Janice. How are you this morning?"

Janice paused in the application of her lipstick to smile at him. "Great. How 'bout you?"

"Fantastic."

Lunch in the fridge, coffee in hand, access the cube and log on, pull together a few files and check out today's word on the vocabulary builder:

Amelioration - (amee-lior-ayshun) n. The action of making better; the being made better; an improvement.

"The repair was an amelioration of the... no, the renovation was an amelioration of the look of the house."

"Morning, Marty. You're babbling a bit early today, aren't you?"

"Morning, Dave."

As soon as the system was live, he checked the claims screen to see if there was a second claim entered for Ultimate Diecasting. But, nothing. Just the first one, and the reserve had been increased to $575 grand! He quickly made his way over to the claims area and Jason's cube, knocking on the partition wall just as he was hanging up the phone.

"Hi, Jason. What's with the reserve increase?"

"And good morning to you. I assume you mean on Ultimate Fly-casting?"

"Yes," said Martin. He shifted his weight from one foot to the other and put his hands in his pockets to keep them still.

"He showed me the books. That contract was worth a half mil. And it's going to cost a bundle to duplicate the plans from old records, not to mention the time required. It's gonna be a huge B.I. loss."

The B.I., or Business Interruption loss, would probably have to be paid. Unless they could prove that the contract was for something military or high hazard which would constitute non-disclosure. If somebody had a fire or a break-in, and as a result they were unable to carry on business for awhile, not only did the insurance company have to pay for the damaged or stolen goods, but also for the profit the insured lost while they couldn't carry on business. As long as they had that coverage on their policy, which this file did, unfortunately.

"Who was the contract for?"

"He wouldn't tell me. Guards that like it was gold."

"I've noticed that," said Martin. "It's got to be something military."

"Yeah, that's what I was thinking. Everything so top secret. But his documentation is sufficient for his proof of loss. I've already talked to his lawyer."

"How's the investigation going?"

"Good. It seems pretty legit. I don't get the sense of it being an inside job. This guy would never risk that. He's definitely P.O.'d that this mess has occurred, and he's told me it jeopardizes his future contracts."

Martin's brow tightened. "Oh. I was thinking that it might have been an inside job."

"Yeah, I thought that was what you were implying the other day. So I did take statements from most of the key staff, and apart from one nervous nellie, nothing much came of it."

"What about this nervous nellie?"

"Oh, the shop supervisor. He just acted really nervous about my questions, and didn't like having to give a statement. Asked me did I think he'd robbed the place. A few red flags, but he had an alibi. Bowling night and then home to the wife. Seemed very confident about that, and the wife confirmed it. I think he's just a nutbar. Paranoid case. You sometimes see that type, and you have to weed them out."

"Interesting. What was his name?"

Jason checked his file. "Tom Peterson."

"Thanks."

Jason was all right when you got him alone, without an audience. Martin knew he cared about his job and enjoyed the investigative side of claims. He was capable of a few civil words at times. Especially at home, Martin thought as he walked back to his desk. He spoke fondly of his young son, who he looked after on weekends since the divorce. An enigma. The sarcastic exterior was probably some kind of defense mechanism.

What Jason had said had given Martin an idea, but he wanted to talk to George first before he tried anything. He went back to his desk and pulled out the card for Matrix Messenger Service.

"Hello, Matrix dispatcher."

"Hi, it's Martin Porchnik calling," he said, mentioning the name of his company.

"Hi, Martin. You've got a rush pickup?"

"No, I need to talk to George, one of your couriers. Can you get a message to him?"

"I could put a call out on the radio. What's the message?"

"Call Martin at this number," he said, giving him the number.

"Okay, got it. I'll do it right now."

"Thanks a lot." He hung up. The business card for Ultimate Diecasting was in the inspection file, so he tore it out and put it in his pocket. George called back within ten minutes.

"Hi, Marty. What's up?"

"George. I was wondering if you could meet me after lunch. I have an idea about our case that I want to run by you."

What's next?

George sat in a Tim Horton's sipping black coffee and resisting the urge to have a maple donut. His body might be a temple, but that didn't mean he was totally celibate. He could resist anything except Timtation, as Oscar Wilde would surely have said if he were in his place. Another five minutes and the donut would be a necessity for his survival.

He hadn't seen his brother in months. It was a busy time of year for Peter, and he had reluctantly agreed to meet him "just for a coffee." And the fact that he was late showed that they were meeting on his time. George had expected as much, and could hardly believe he had called him. It really galled him that he was even considering this.

All he ever heard from his parents was about his expensive university education and how after all that he was just a bicycle messenger. Look at your brother Peter, he's doing better than you and he never even went to college. When are you going to show some ambition? Do something constructive with your life?

But Peter had never bugged him about it. He was easy-going, affable. Never had any big dreams as a kid, just wanted to make a decent living, have a lot of friends, wife, kids, the whole deal. And he got exactly that. George guessed there was a benefit to knowing what you wanted. Or maybe it was in wanting simple things.

Peter arrived then. An inch shorter than George, but with a more muscular upper body, and much shorter hair. He wore khaki shorts and a white t-shirt under a navy work shirt with his company name stitched on it. Looking tired and sweaty but still clean-shaven and professional.

"Hey, Pete!" He waved him over as he came in the door.

"Hey, little brother. Is that a new earring?"

"No, same as last time," George said as he stood up to give Pete a hug. "You getting a coffee?"

"No time," said Pete, although he sat down as if it felt really good to do so.

"C'mon. Take five minutes. I'm buying."

"Well, in that case. Make it a fancy café mocha or something."

George was next in line when his phone burbled with Chuck putting out a call. Shit, he hated to miss a pick-up. He pulled it off his belt and switched off the 2-way radio part and switched his phone to silent.

With an English Toffee Cappuccino in tow, George returned to the table to get on with it. "So, how's business?"

Pete pulled the cup over in front of him and took a sip. "Busy as all hell. Which is why I don't like to meet in the afternoon. Gotta make hay while the sun shines, know what I mean?"

"Yeah. So, listen. I've been thinking about your offer."

"You've gotta be kidding. I never thought I'd hear you say that. I thought Gina was pregnant or something. That's fantastic! I always said we'd make a great team. When can you start, 'cause I could really use an extra hand right now."

"Not so fast. We're just talking about possibilities here. I like the idea of working outside, and I don't mind hard work, but I can't be all about mowing lawns and clipping hedges."

"Well, that's the business, my son. What'd you think you'd be doing?"

"That's what I wanted to talk about. I have a little money saved up, and I was hoping you'd let me buy in as a partner for some of the start-up costs."

"What start-up costs?"

"I was thinking we could take the business in a new direction. I'd like to get into landscape design. Maybe look at doing custom decks and gazebos. We could offer the whole package: design, build and service."

Pete sipped at his coffee and surveyed George's face. "And you'll hack it out on the laptop while I do the heavy lifting, eh?"

"Not at all. I want to be involved in all aspects of the business. I'm not afraid to get my hands dirty, and I love working in the great outdoors.

Pete laughed. "I was only pullin' your chain."

"We'd just sub out the labor for the actual building

part of it, or eventually take on some carpenters. For all our customers on the design and build, we could give them a discount on ongoing lawn maintenance and eventually pick up quite a client list. And vice versa for your existing customers. Give them all a brochure and offer to quote on a job."

"Yeah, give 10% off the usual rate. Maybe a little something for referrals, too. That could work." He drank about half his coffee in one long swallow and sat there nodding for a second. "This is quite an idea, Georgey. Let me think about it. Mull it over some. Why don't you put some numbers together for me and we'll talk about it on Sunday. You and Gina come for dinner."

"Great. You won't be disappointed."

"No, I don't believe I will. You're not going to try to turn me into an archie-tectural firm, now, are ya?"

"Couldn't do it even if I wanted to."

Peter laughed again and stood up. "Gotta get back at it. But you've really intrigued me, here. This idea is growing on me."

"Just you wait. See you Sunday, Pete."

"See you."

Damn, his parents were going to love this one. Which was the biggest downside of the whole idea. He had become comfortable with his role as a disappointment. George gulped the last of his barely warm coffee and was feeling so pleased with himself, he got another one, and a maple donut.

Lunch Date

Martin could hardly concentrate at work with all
that had gone on. The excitement of the previous
night was still flowing through his veins, combined
with the impatience to try out his new idea. He had
witnessed an actual break-in, had followed the
burglars in his car, had done some detective work
with George and found out things that no one else
knew about this case. No closer to figuring it out, but
damn what a thrill ride! For god's sake, he couldn't
be 38. He felt like a little kid.

For most of the morning since he'd called George,
he had pushed papers around his desk, trying to look
busy. He looked at the inspection file on 50 Silver
Star Boulevard and relived it all several times, as well
as going over all the pieces of information as if he
could eventually manipulate them enough so that
they'd fall into place and reveal that which was now
hidden. He couldn't make the connection, but he had
an idea that might shake a new piece loose.

By the time lunch rolled around, he had done
essentially no work, but felt immensely pleased with
himself nonetheless. He logged off the computer and

went into the lunch room. Opening the fridge to gaze in at his paper sack sitting on the top shelf all by itself, it struck him that today was not a bag lunch day. Today was a going out for lunch day, definitely. He closed the fridge, grabbed his jacket from his desk chair, and walked towards the front door, passing Dave on his way out.

"Where you going, Marty?"

Martin stopped and turned around. "Out."

"Out for lunch? No ham and swiss on rye?"

"Nope," said Martin, standing up a little straighter and trying to suck in his belly.

"Then, the dream is over. The chain has been broken. Let the Four Horsemen of the Apocalypse ride tonight, for this is the day that Martin Porchnik gets his lunch on the outside. Can I have your sandwich?"

"Sure. It's in the fridge."

"Thanks. I want to have it bronzed. Do you think bronzed ham will keep?"

The double doors seemed to swing open at his very touch, for surely he was destiny's child now. When he rounded the corner by the elevators, he saw Janice was already waiting.

She looked up when she heard his footsteps behind her. "Oh. Hi, Marty. Got some errands to do?"

"Nope, I'm going out for lunch," he said.

"No way. I don't think I've ever seen you go out for lunch. Where you going?"

"I don't know, yet."

"Mind if I join you?"

"Not at all."

At that moment, the elevator door opened, and an oppressive bank of stares instantly silenced them. Martin stood uncomfortably beside Janice for 46 floors while people got on and off. His previous confidence quickly evaporated in the tense social jelly of the elevator dynamic and he wondered what he had been thinking when he decided to go out for lunch. Now he was going out to eat with Janice. That wasn't the same as eating in with Janice. What did it mean? Was this just a co-worker thing? Just, you know, casual? He wasn't good at these kinds of situations. His pits started getting all juiced up.

When they finally tumbled off the elevator on the ground floor, he was a ball of insecurity and various neuroses. He had to break the silence or die trying.

"I'm new at this. Where's a good place to eat?" *Perfect. Very safe.*

"There's always the food court, or we could go somewhere a little different."

"It's up to you." *Indecisive. Jelly-fish.*

"What do you feel like?"

"Salad." *What did he mean, salad? He never ate salad.*

"Okaaay, we could go to the Richtree Market. They do a nice salad."

"Great. It's not expensive, is it?" *Stupid, stupid, stupid...*

"Not too bad. Just watch how many stamps you get, because they really add up."

They walked along King and then down Yonge towards the restaurant, Martin careful to take the outside like a gentleman. Grabbing trays at the door, they wandered from station to station, choosing this item and that, all freshly prepared, and having their passports stamped each time. Food in hand, they finally found a window seat on the Yonge Street side.

"You were right," said Martin. "They had a great selection of salads."

"I didn't realize you were so health conscious."

"Yeah, well, it's important to be healthy. It's better than the alternative."

"So true. How's that Caesar?"

"Delicious. Good soup?"

"Mmm, yeah," said Janice, wiping her mouth on her napkin. "It's my favorite."

"So, uh, how are things with you?"

"Oh, they're okay. My mom's been having a hard time lately, so I've been looking after her. Breast cancer."

"Oh, no. That's awful."

"It really is. I've been taking her to the chemo treatments and they just leave her so weak and sickly."

"Sounds nasty. She's lucky to have you. What if you had a family to look after?"

"I think I'd still be there for her. Since my Dad died, I'm all she's got."

"You're a good daughter, single or married, then."

"Oh, speaking of single. Did you hear that Darlene and her boyfriend broke up?"

"No. When did this happen?"

"Last week."

"Nobody tells me anything. What happened?" said Martin. *Why didn't Darlene mention this to him? Weird. He thought they were pretty friendly.*

"He just told her it was over. He'd met someone else."

"Oh, no. Poor Darlene. But better she found out he was a bastard sooner than later."

"True. She's too young to be tied down anyway."

"Yeah, she'll bounce back. She's not old and jaded like us."

"Hey, what do you mean, old? Speak for yourself, Gramps."

"Sorry, I just meant old-er."

"Yeah, yeah. What about you, old-timer, you dating anyone?"

"Nope. Not me."

They munched in silence for a few moments. Janice was okay. Even a comment she could have taken offense at she blew off like it was nothing. Which was a good thing, because he was infamous for saying the wrong thing at the wrong time.

"So, are you going to the company picnic?" she asked him.

"No way. I went a couple of times years ago, but it just seemed to be aimed at people with kids. No thanks."

"It's not that bad. Free food and get some time to actually have a conversation with your co-workers. It's nice."

Martin nodded and chewed. Lunch seemed to fly past as they talked about this and that, what books they were reading, laughed a few times. It was very comfortable. Neither of them had anything to prove to the other and they'd known each other for years. Maybe never gone out for lunch together, but had countless inconsequential conversations, so it came rather easily. When they were finished, they lined up to hand in their passports and pay the piper.

"Seventeen dollars!" he complained when they were outside. "Now I remember why I never go out for lunch."

"A couple of dollars for your coffee, a dollar for your roll, and then tax on top. It adds up in a hurry. I don't go there every day, but it's a nice treat."

"It was good," he admitted.

They re-entered their building and again rode the elevator in silence to the 46th floor. Janice spoke first when they got off. "That was fun. We should do it again sometime. Or was that it for this year?"

"This decade."

"Oh, well, then. See you again in ten years?"

"Yeah, but next time, let's do the food court. My budget can't take this beating every ten years."

"We could just get a hot dog at the vendor across the road."

"Now that's more my speed."

He smiled and waved a 'see ya later' at Janice and got a nice smile in return. Janice the hottie. The lunch date had given him lots of warm tingly feelings and, wait just a second, was he calling it a date? It was accidental to begin with and he was much too comfortable talking to her for it to have been a real date. Just the thought of real dates made his throat dry up and had him tripping up on carpet and trying to decide how to walk. Did he swing his arms as much when he walked during his normal, non-date life?

Besides, they were from two different worlds. Janice was a Receptionist. Hers was the rough and tumble world of buzzing phones and impatient people waiting for meetings. Angry phone calls and disappointed claimants. He was a Commercial Underwriter. Top of the food chain in the heady world of business risk assessment and rate divination. Coffee drinking and computer eye strain. She was a normal, good-looking person. He was a rumpled, balding hermit with no pictures on his walls. What was he going to do, just pick her up in a ten-year-old Toyota Tercel? The Beige Bomber? Best to put Janice out of his mind.

But he couldn't.

One Nervous Nellie

A look at the clock told him he only had another twenty minutes until he had to scoot downstairs to Starbucks to meet George. He hadn't done a lick of work today. The only thing that might fit into twenty minutes was checking and returning voice mail, which he did with the confidence and authority of someone who went on lunch dates with attractive women. His voice sounded different to him, more self-assured. Did the brokers notice? He hung up the phone at about three minutes to 2:00, grabbed his jacket off the back of his chair and walked to the front door.

Janice looked at him quizzically. "You're going out again?"

"Yeah, I'm just meeting George for coffee."

"Oh. Well, say hi for me."

"Will do."

There wasn't much elevator traffic on the way down at that time of day, he noted. He seemed to get down in record time, emerging into the underground Path and turning the corner towards Starbucks. By some miracle, George had chosen the right one and he waved to Martin from the line-up. Really? A line-up at 2:00? To buy five dollar coffee? This is why he never went out.

"Hey, big guy," said George. "What kind of frou-frou coffee do you want?" He was wearing his usual Matrix Messenger shirt and bike shorts and had his bike seat hanging off his satchel at his back.

"One that doesn't cost five dollars."

"Oh, you mean Tim Horton's coffee. I've already had one of those today."

"They have to have regular coffee here." Martin searched the menu board.

"Yeah, they do." George reached the head of the line and moved forward to place his order. "One grande café misto with soy."

"Jesus, that's regular?" said Martin. "Can I just have a regular coffee, please?"

The coffee lady pressed buttons on her computer and smiled at him reassuringly. "Yes, of course. Mild, medium or bold?"

"What the what?"

"Do you prefer lighter or stronger flavor?" Her fingers hovered over the buttons, just waiting for him to utter his choice. Why did the coffee smell burnt? How could they get away with selling coffee made from beans they had burned? The menu board behind her was filled with options, none of which purported to be regular coffee. She also had big boobs underneath her green apron, which he was having a hard time keeping his eyes off. They were hypnotic.

"Medium, regular, run of the mill," he managed to say as he pulled out his wallet.

"That'll be a Tall House Blend."

"With cream and sugar. And I'm getting both of these," said Martin, indicating George's coffee and his own.

"Cream and sugar is right behind you, sir. That'll be $7.87."

He gave her the money, not caring at this point what it cost, as long as he could get away from the glare of her teeth and her tempting eye candy.

"Thanks, Martin," said George. "C'mon over here with me. We wait by this little counter thingy. She just takes the orders."

"Wow, this is a weird place. No wonder I never come here."

"The coffee is great, though."

"Twice as good as Timmies? Because it's twice the price."

"Yeah, I guess. So, what's your idea?"

He told him about his conversation with Jason about the shop supervisor and the big contracts on the books. Their coffees arrived and they mixed and stirred them and then sat at a small table by a wall of windows.

"Wow, so that guy is obviously the contact," said George. "Is that what you were thinking?"

"Exactly. He could have told them where the plans were kept, when the contract came in, all that stuff. He's in the perfect position."

"So, we know the goon's room number. We could

just call them and tell them we know who their contact is and that we're going to rat them out to the police. See what they do."

"I was thinking more along the lines of calling the contact and pretending to be the goons, see if we can scare him into doing something foolish. You could call and disguise your voice."

"Yeah! I can imitate those guys perfectly. All you do is curse with every other word and talk like your nose has been blocked for about 18 years."

"So what should we tell him?" said Martin. He tried to think it through.

"We can tell him we're going to hurt him if he doesn't deliver the goods, personally. Make him drop off the new contract, set up a meeting place."

"Then we call the goons and tell them the same meeting place and time?"

"Right. Then we tip the cops to the whole thing and catch them in the act."

"But what if they contact each other in the meantime? They might set up a different time, and then we look like idiots and the whole thing gets messy."

"Oh, yeah," said George.

"It would be simpler if we got the contact to entice them to come down and break in again."

"You're right. Then we could stake the place out and call the cops as soon as they break in."

Martin nodded. "Riiight. What if we told the contact that we knew about the whole thing and we were going to take it to the cops unless he co-operated? He could tell them that the new contract is in, and exactly where the plans are locked up. The goons already think the place is easy to break into. They wouldn't hesitate to hit it again."

"Perfect! Man, you're a natural at this."

"It's all the detective novels I've been reading. They must have rubbed off. But who do I tell him I am when I'm calling?"

"Tell him who you are. It'll sound more official if you work for the insurance company. Tell him you work with the cops on these investigations. He'd better co-operate if he didn't want to go down with them. Mention Mr. Smith."

Martin thought it through and nodded, despite the small chill of fear that was starting to climb its way out of his gut. "That could work."

"What have we got to lose?"

"What if he gives my name to the goons?"

"He'll be so scared of the police, he'll go along with it. He's just a regular Joe Lunchpail, wife and kids at home, who got offered a little extra cash for some information. He doesn't want this to come out. Have his name in the paper. Play up that stuff. If he was a real criminal hard case, he would've done the job himself."

"True. But it's still a risk."

"It's up to you. We could just hand everything that we know over to the police and wash our hands of it."

"No, I want to catch these bastards, like you said. I'll give it a try."

"This is too much. I swear, you're the coolest, Marty."

"I am cool. Just call me a rebel without a clause, I guess."

George looked at him with no hint of comprehension. "Huh?"

"That's insurance humor. Clause, get it?"

"Yeah, sure, that's a real laugh, Marty."

"But I'm still cool, right?"

"Frozen, baby. Chatter your teeth. Sub-zero."

"Now all I have to do is not chatter my teeth on the phone. My hands are sweating just thinking of it. I have very active sweat glands."

"You'll be fine. But good luck all the same."

"By the way, this is an unrelated thing, but do you know where I could get a good haircut? Something with a little more style?"

"Yeah, sure. That could be step one in the makeover. Gina goes to this place on Yonge called Civello's. A lot of people from the ad agency go there, and it is the ultimate in stylish."

"Where is it on Yonge?"

"It's near the Canadian Tire, just north of Bloor."

"Okay. Civello's. Thanks a lot. I'll check it out this weekend."

"Tell them you want a change. Not just the same old, same old."

"Okay, I'd better get back to the office."

"Yeah, I've got to get back on the road."

George drank his last sip of coffee and stood to leave. "Let me know how it goes. Here's my cell number, so you don't have to dispatch me again. It's not a very private way to send a message. Everyone hears the dispatch." He handed him a scrap of paper.

"Let me give you mine. I'll write it on the back of one of my cards." He wrote out the number and handed him the card. "Thanks for all your help on this. I never would have come this far without you. I would have sat in my cubicle and worried, like I always do."

"No problem. I'm always up for endangering lives." George smiled widely and walked off in the direction of the escalators to the outside world, his bike seat bobbing along behind him. Martin walked back to the elevators and waited with a crowd. He couldn't help feeling elated about all this scheming and manipulating. He got on the elevator thinking he had a shot at pulling all this off. As he was on his way down the hall back to the office, he passed Janice coming the other way, probably on her way to the washrooms.

"Hi, Martin."

Something clicked at the sight of her walking along by herself out here, this moment alone together somehow connected to the good feelings of their lunch today and the high of his newfound boldness. He turned.

"Hi, Janice," he said. "I was just, um..." So embarrassing. How did this go again? Where was that confidence he'd felt a few seconds ago?

Janice waited expectantly. "Yes?"

Some kind of fear reflex sprung up into his brain all

on its own. The *Danger!* warnings were all there: he'd been down this road before, it went nowhere, it would all end in pain, he was not cut out for a relationship, it would have happened by now if it was going to, she would tear his heart out and feed it to him for breakfast, it was too big a risk. But what had his life been like since he stopped taking risks? Safe? Boring. Well, not exactly boring when you consider... Oh, what the hell.

"I was wondering..." he said. He started again. "Janice, I had a lot of fun getting lunch with you today. Would you like to go out with me sometime? For real, I mean?"

She laughed. "For real? You mean like on a date?"

Hers was a nice laugh. "Yes."

"Sure, Martin. I'd love to."

He breathed out all at once and smiled at this unexpected happy outcome. Now who said what? It had been a long time since Martin had done any of this. "So, this Friday night? Dinner?"

"Sounds good."

"Good. Yes. How about I pick you up at around 7:00?"

"Sure. You'll need, um, why don't I just e-mail you my address and cell phone number?"

"Great." He didn't know what to do with his hands, so he put one in his pocket and patted his thigh with the other. He felt like he was posing for a Sears catalog photo. "So, I'll just head back to my desk."

"Great. And thanks for asking."

"Okay," said Martin. He smiled and moved past her, back to his desk, wondering how this all happened. Against all odds he had asked her, and against all odds she had said yes. Maybe he asked her because he thought she would say no, all flirty and single as she was. He half expected that she would say she already had a boyfriend. But this was perfect. All those lunches together. There was a comfort factor there and he needed to feel comfortable or he would be a basket case. No, this was good. He was going on a date with his friend, Janice.

George Gives Notice

Before going to finish off his afternoon pickups, George biked down to the Matrix office to see his dispatcher and de facto employer, Chuck Robinson, although all the couriers were like independents, in a way. They would also pick up other work here and there, but all had their own regular route in the afternoons. Chuck called the pickups from a small storefront setup over on Parliament just north of Queen, a converted house.

"Knock-knock."

"George, how are ya? C'mon in. What's up?"

"My time."

"How's that?"

"I've come to give you my notice."

"Yeah, right. What is it? A money thing? You want more calls?"

"No, I'm serious. I've got no complaints, I appreciate the job you've provided me for over three years, but it's just time to do something new."

"Well, that's really classy of you, GG. I never got notice before. Usually a guy doesn't show up two days in a row, that's my notice. How long you givin' me?"

"A week."

"More than enough. I'm really sorry to lose you, but I have to confess, I was just waiting for this day. You're too smart for this stuff. A lot of these guys, they're lucky to have this at all. But you could be doing something better. Got any plans?"

"Yeah, I'm going into business with my brother."

"Oh, an entrepreneur, are we? Well, all the best to you. Good luck with it. Call me if you need any deliveries."

"Will do. See you later."

"See you. And hey, George. You were right, my cholesterol count was up. Results from a recent check-up. I'm eating oat bran, now."

"Stick with it, Chuck."

"I will."

He stuck the toe of his shoe into the pedal clip and kicked his leg over the bike as it was already rolling and pedaled away down Parliament to King and then over. Now to make it through the last week alive.

The Phone Call

Back at his desk, Martin organized his thoughts for the upcoming phone call. He even made some notes, planning the conversation in detail. None of this 'see what happens.' He liked to be prepared. He set out the business card and the book of matches George had given him. He thought about what he would say and how he would use the information he had. When he felt ready, he dialed the number.

"Good afternoon, Ultimate Diecasting."

"Hello, may I speak to Tom, please?"

"Just a moment, please."

"Thanks." Martin tapped his pen on the pad of paper in front of him while he waited.

"Hello, Tom Peterson."

"Hello, Mr. Peterson. My name is Martin Porchnik. I am an underwriter with the insurance company that is handling a claim for Ultimate Diecasting."

"What's an 'underwriter?'"

"It's a kind of company investigator."

"Oh, yeah. Well, I've already talked to one of your investigators, so don't bother. I don't have anything else to say."

"We know you set it all up, Mr. Peterson." Martin held his breath.

"What?"

"It was you. You set it up."

"I don't know what you're talking about, and I don't have time for this kind of bullshit. I'm hanging up n—"

"We know you told them about the contract and where to find the plans."

"What a load of crap. If you don't stop harassing me, I'm going to call the police. I've had about as much as I'm going to take."

"Go ahead. We're working in conjunction with the police on this matter. It's not you that we're after. We want the big fish. If you help us catch them, the police don't have to know about your involvement."

"There is no involvement. I wasn't involved in anything. Except answering stupid questions."

"Mr. Peterson. It's all going to come out. They're going to be caught and the whole story will come out. I don't think your wife wants to see your name in the paper."

Silence.

"You want to see your kids only on visiting days? Introduce them to your new friends in the slammer?"

Martin paused. Maybe 'slammer' was too old-fashioned. It was the term that Mickey Spillane used and those books were pretty old. Oh, well. He'd get the gist of it.

"I don't know anything about this. I'll be calling

my lawyer."

"Tom, we know about you and Mr. Smith."

Silence. Martin prayed he'd got it right. He could feel the pulsing of blood in his temples as he pressed the phone to his ear. Then he heard a sigh on the line like the wind slowly going out of a balloon.

"Oh, my god. I should've known it would come out. It was all going so well. But when I saw those FBI guys here yesterday, I knew the shit would hit the fan."

"FBI?"

"Yeah, on account of the nuclear contract with the DOD. This is news to you?"

"No, of course not."

Martin panicked. FBI? DOD? Nuclear? It didn't matter. Just focus, push on through and think about it later. "Anyway, it doesn't have to come out, if you co-operate."

"Shit. What choice do I have? Okay, let's hear it."

"It's very simple. Do you have a piece of paper?"

"Just a second. Okay. Go ahead."

"You're going to call this number." Martin picked up the book of matches from the Holiday Inn and read it off to him. "And ask for room number 725. Seven-Two-Five. You will be talking to one of the men who broke in."

"Jesus, you know where they're staying?"

"We know a lot more than that."

"Okay, I've got it. What do I say?"

"You're going to say that the new contract just came in and then tell them exactly where the plans can be found. Tell them they're locked up tighter than a drum. They'll scoff at that."

"Where should I tell them they'll be?"

"I don't care. Make it up. They're going to be caught before they've had a chance to figure it out."

"And that's it? What if they ask how I got their number? You don't think they're going to be curious?"

"Tell them Mr. Smith gave you the number."

"What if he tells them he didn't?"

Good point. Martin improvised. "He's not around right now to tell them."

"Okay. When do you want me to call?"

"Tonight. We can't waste any more time. These guys are itching to get out of town."

"All right. I hope you know what you're doing."

"I do."

"And my part in this will never come out?"

"You have my word."

"All right."

"Oh, by the way, Mr. Peterson."

"Yeah?"

"Use a fake name. I don't think these two know who you are, and they don't need to know."

"Good idea."

"Good luck."

Martin hung up the phone. Man, that felt good. His pulse was racing, but it had gone perfectly. Nothing could have gone any smoother. His plan might just work after all. And the contract was with the Department of Defense. Nuclear arms? From a product liability point of view, he was horrified. But as for the rest, it was too much! His own life had become more exciting than the best mystery thriller he'd ever read. No wonder these guys were so determined to get the plans. Someone wanted to build their own nuclear weapons.

Turning to his computer, he brought up the Internet browser and switched from the company web page to the Google site. His curiosity was piqued about how a Toronto machine shop got involved in the nuclear industry. Why would the U.S. Government deal with a Canadian manufacturer? Or any manufacturer? Didn't they make that stuff themselves?

First he searched for 'nuclear weapons canada.' Much to his surprise, Canada was in the nuclear business right from the start. Britain and Canada both helped the U.S. on the original Manhattan Project. He knew that Canada was a world leader in producing radioactive isotopes for medical purposes, as it had been in the news a while back, but he had thought that was just a by-product of their nuclear energy program. The nuclear industry itself in Canada dated back to 1942, when construction on the first nuclear reactor began. It was the most powerful research reactor in the world when it was completed.

There was a lot of peaceful energy stuff to be found, but what about the bloody bombs? Next he searched for 'nuclear weapons manufacturing,' and had to learn the difference between atomic bombs and hydrogen bombs, nuclear fission and nuclear fusion. Nuclei were either splitting apart or bashing into each other, apparently. All the different materials: uranium, plutonium, deuterium, hydrogen, and tritium. He had heard most of these terms before. Pop culture or Dr. Strangelove? He just wasn't finding what he was looking for. Did the Canadian government have the bomb and he'd just never heard about it? What would be happening in Canada that some bad guy or bad government would want to get a hold of?

Finally, something caught his eye under a web page which mentioned manufacturing of nuclear weapons: *"Producing highly enriched uranium entails many steps apart from the enrichment process itself and many other installations and capabilities are necessary. Nations wishing to obtain highly enriched uranium without international restrictions prohibiting its use for nuclear explosives would have to develop enrichment technology independently, or obtain it illegally, since virtually all nuclear exporter states are unwilling to sell nuclear equipment and materials."* The Carnegie Endowment on Nuclear Manufacturing. Dale Carnegie was into nukes? That guy had his finger in every pie.

How to build an atomic bomb was apparently no big secret. He'd just found all the plans he would need. The technology was challenging enough, but the real key was building giant, stable reactors in which to enrich the uranium or plutonium you would need for the fissile material required to produce the explosion. The world leader in giant, stable reactors was Canada. We don't have the bomb, we have the fuel-makers. And someone wanted to make some fuel and blow somebody up. Well, not on Martin Porchnik's watch, mister. Not while his company was on risk!

This was wicked cool. Who could he call to tell about all this?

What time was it? Maybe he'd try calling George, at least leave a message and tell him how well it had gone. As he reached for the phone, his direct line began to ring. He picked it up by force of habit.

"Hello, Martin Porchnik speaking."

"Martin, are you some kind of cop?"

"What? No, I'm an underwriter," he said automatically.

"Oh, yeah? What's an 'underwriter?'"

Martin paused. Was this Tom Peterson's way of checking up on him?

"It's a kind of company investigator."

"An investigator, huh? And have you been talking to George about your little investigation there?"

"George? Yeah. How do you know George? Who is this?"

At that point, Big Eddy hung up the phone.

That was odd, thought Martin. *How could Peterson know about George?* Nobody knew he'd been talking to him about this. Maybe it was someone from the courier service where he'd given his name. He hoped that was all it was. He hoped that it hadn't spoiled the set-up.

He picked up the phone and dialed George's

number, but got his voice mail. He couldn't just leave all this on a message, so he just told him how things went with Tom and about his plans for the evening. How was he going to be able to wait till evening when he was this excited already?

The Other Phone Call

Mr. Smith sat back in his chair and observed his two associates sitting across the table from him. He crossed his arms and inhaled slowly before beginning.

"What we have is not sufficient. There is more to this, and we cannot deliver it incomplete. Our buyer will be seriously displeased at this paucity of information. The whole contract might be canceled, and I do not just mean financially. You have no idea with whom you are dealing."

"But we looked everywhere. I'm tellin' ya, I know those files better than the effin secretary."

"And that's another point. Why can't ya tell us who it is we're dealing with, Smitty? Because I'm getting pretty fuckin' tired of listening to you. Maybe I should be dealing directly with the buyer."

"Nothing would give me greater pleasure than to see you dealing directly with this party, but sadly, that's not in my best interests. Or yours."

"Take it easy, the both of you. What are we going to do about this? Maybe we should be talking to our so-called 'contact,' who doesn't seem like he gave us the whole story."

"Yeah, that little fucker scammed us from the start, and is probably spending our money right now. Let me talk to him for five minutes and the bastard will be drawing us the plans from memory."

"That's not going to—"

The phone started ringing.

"Who the fuck is that gonna be?"

Mr. Smith folded his arms with a wry smile on his face. "Well, why not just pick up the phone and find out?"

"Yeah?"

"Hi, this is Rick Savage."

"Who the fuck?"

"Your contact. I talked to Mr. Smith before."

"Well, well, you little prick. We were just talking about ya. Now you're gonna tell me who gave you this number before I come and beat it out of you."

"It was Mr. Smith."

"Oh, yeah? (The guy's saying you gave him this number. Is that right? Hello? I said, is that right?)"

"Yes, that is correct."

"Okay, then, Mister Savage. Let's hear what ya got, cause I'm about ready to come and bust in your head with a ratchet, just for the aggravation ya caused me."

"Okay, I'm sorry. The new contract is in. I can tell you where to find the plans you want."

"That's better. Where do I find them, and I mean tell me exactly where."

"It's in a document safe, in the office, behind the locked files. The files are a dummy. The safe is built into the wall and bolted down."

"Why the fuck didn't you tell us this before?"

"They just put it in yesterday. The place was crawling with FBI. You'd better be careful; I think they've beefed up security."

"I sure hope they have, because it was pretty fucking pathetic before. But I'm touched that you'd worry about us like that."

"Now this information is above and beyond what we agreed before, and I think I should be paid extra. I've put myself at great personal risk."

"Yeah, sure. The check's in the mail. Made out to Prick Savage, Bank of Fuck You."

"That was hardly a cordial way to hang up on a man who has served us so well."

"Whatever. I get the feeling he's still jerking us around. Why would he tell us all that without getting the money up front like last time?"

"Because I asked him to. I can be very persuasive."

"What about that name? Isn't 'Rick Savage' a porn star name or something?"

"Yes, that's very astute. It was a fake name."

"Well, what's his real name, in case I wanna drop in on him?"

"You need not know that. Let us concentrate on the task at hand, gentlemen. Payday is almost upon us, and then you will both be very rich men."

"Now you're talking. When."

"I think tonight. Before they have a chance to put any more security in place."

"Sounds good to me. I'm getting pretty sick of

sitting around, tell you the truth."

Captured

"Courier," George said.

"Just be a minute, they're packaging it now," said the receptionist of a Bay Street accounting firm on George's route.

While he waited, he ran through ideas for the business. He would need a new laptop, one capable of running AutoCAD or similar programs. That would be the main expense, apart from advertising, and initial printing runs for invoices, letterhead, and, of course, business cards. He could finally put those letters he had earned after his name when they would actually mean something. He'd be the most overqualified landscape designer in the city, but who cares?

Pete had a smart head for business. George would have to learn to rely on him for most of that. He was great at keeping expenses low and keeping track of the logistics. He had made a successful business out of a lawn mower and a rake at the age of 18.

"Here you go, George. Take it easy."

"Thanks." On with the Ray-Bans and out the door. The elevator let him out at the ground floor, and he pushed his way through the revolving doors and out onto the sidewalk towards his bike. He barely had time to notice the large brown van parked next to it when he felt someone grab him by the arm. He struggled against the powerful grip, but his satchel was almost immediately taken off his shoulder and he saw Chet hop on his bike and speed away with it. Turning his head around to see who his captor was, he found himself face to face with Big Eddy.

"You've been avoiding me, Georgey."

"No, I've just been busy. I was going to come see you tonight."

"You've been a real fleet-footed Hermes to catch up with, too. But now we're going to go and have a little talk."

The van door swung open and George was pulled in by someone inside. The sunglasses were ripped off his face and a sack was thrown over his head. Something hard hit him across the back and he fell to the floor of the van. His hands were bound with some kind of rough twine. Two doors slammed shut and they were moving.

His heart beat wildly but he forced himself to control his breathing. If he kept on hyperventilating in the sack he would quickly pass out. Once he had calmed his breathing, he tried to listen for clues as to where they were going, but apart from traffic sounds, he could hear nothing.

"C'mon Eddy, can't we just—" he began, but was cut off by a sudden blow to his kidney. Nobody spoke again for the entire journey.

George's mind worked over what he would say, tried to think of what they might do to him. How far would they take this? How much money was involved? Would they just threaten him, or actually try to get rid of him? He didn't think the situation could be all that bad. He didn't really know anything and this was a small time operation, wasn't it? He would agree to whatever they said, not provoke them, and hope like hell he could talk his way out of it.

The ride seemed to last forever. His concept of time was skewed in his current condition, but he suspected it was between 45 minutes and an hour before they pulled to a stop. Someone got out of the van and slammed the door closed. He heard a roll-up door opening. The van drove forward and then the sound of the door rolling closed again. Another door opened in the van and the sliding door was pulled open. Someone inside the van pulled him up and pushed him towards someone else waiting outside the van.

Someone was holding his arm and pushing him forward. He heard a door being opened in front of them and closing behind them once they had passed through. He was suddenly turned around and pushed down from the shoulders. A chair impeded his downward progress, and the sack was removed. His hands and legs were secured to the chair.

The first thing he saw was Big Eddy right in front of him, tying one of his feet. He was still dressed in Gold's Gym sweats and his bicycle shorts and shoes.

Obviously this grab had been put together in a hurry.

Taking a quick look around, he found himself in an industrial-type building, but not a very big area. Bare concrete block walls, exposed electrical fixtures, and no furniture, save for a couple of chairs and a table over by one wall. There was another man standing by the table with his arms crossed. He wore jeans, a black turtleneck, and black leather jacket. And he was wearing George's Ray-Bans.

Eddy paced around after tying him up, and then finally spoke. "Well, well. I've been very worried about you, Georgey. I've been thinking a lot about you. Wondering. Thinking."

"There's nothing to worry about."

"So you say. But what am I waiting to hear?"

"I'm... sorry?"

"No, what should I have already heard from you?"

"Oh, yes. I received your generous offer, but I don't think it's right for me. So I'll have to decline."

"Now, was that so hard? I'm a civilized man, George. All I ask is a little civility. And if I'd heard that from you right away, we wouldn't be having this conversation. But things have gotten more complicated since then."

"Nothing's complicated about it, Eddy. Just let me go, and you'll never hear another word about it."

"You know, George, being a courier is dangerous work. A lot of risks involved. You could get hit by a bus on the way home tonight. Or, if not a bus, then a brown van with stolen plates, traveling way too fast."

"I know it's a risky business, Eddy. And that's why

every morning I set up a time-delayed e-mail on my computer. This e-mail tells everything I know about this operation and my potential untimely death. Do you want to guess who it's addressed to? You can check it out, Crime Stoppers is info@222tips.com. As long as I get home okay each night, the e-mail is deleted before it is sent." He hadn't actually done this, but he really wished now that he had done more than just Google Crime Stoppers with a guilty conscience.

"What do you know about our operation, as you call it?" said Eddy sharply.

"Actually," said George. "Not much. Mostly what I assume, but enough to make it hard for you and Chet, at least. Listen, I'm in the dark here. Let's keep it that way. Pretend I have that sack over my head for keeps."

Eddy ignored his plea. "Why would you bother with all that? Time delayed fucking e-mails. Crime Stoppers. We talked to your friend Martin. We know he's investigating us. And we know you're helping him. So how is this e-mail thing any worse than that?"

"What are you talking about? What about Martin?"

"We called him today, and he confirmed everything. Doesn't look too good on you, Georgey-boy."

"Martin works for an insurance company. He's a friend of mine and I have been helping him investigate a break-in that his company paid out money on."

"That's a nice story, George. But it seems like convenient timing that you're telling us this now. Can you see how we would suspect your motivation?"

"What time is it?"

"6:30."

"Okay. Call the same number you heard over the radio. It's Martin's direct line. He won't be there right now, so press zero when you hear his voice, and the call will bounce to the switchboard and you'll hear that what I say is true."

"That's fine, George. I can do that for you. I've got nothing but time here. I'll be back in a minute."

Big Eddy walked over to the door and left the room. The other man remained standing in the corner without saying a thing. George looked at him warily, and wondered about his function in all this. Most of all, he fervently hoped that what he'd said would be true, and there would be a nice recorded message clearly stating the name of the insurance company. But surely they'd have an after-hours claims service? After a few minutes, the door opened again, and Big Eddy returned.

"That's very good, George. I'm impressed. So your story checks out."

"I'm telling you, Eddy. You've got nothing to fear from me. I'm very discreet."

"All right, then. Tell me what I want to hear."

"Besides the fact that I know basically nothing about your operation, except what Chet told me, I'm also quitting the business. As long as nothing happens to me, you'll never hear from me again. And neither will the police."

"That's a good start. I like what I'm hearing. But I'm going to have to hand you over to my colleague here. We'll call him Bob. Bob has a what you might call incentive program to share with you."

The man who'd been lounging against the wall came over to George's chair slowly, his movements languid and unhurried. He hunched a little when he walked. Stopping in front of the chair, he raised his foot to the center of George's chest and slowly pushed him backwards, tipping the chair over, over, over, until it fell back and hit the floor with a wham! The back of George's head hit the concrete and his hands were crushed under his own weight. He blew out a breath through clenched teeth and winced at the pain. The man called Bob crouched down next to him and removed the sunglasses, looking into his eyes, and poking him in the chest for emphasis.

"I'm going to be setting up an Uzi mail for you, bicycle boy. As long as my friends stay out of jail, the message won't be delivered. Do you understand what I'm telling you?"

George nodded his head.

"I will personally see to it that your testicles are fed to my pet iguana."

George nodded again. The man stood, put the shades back on, and returned to his spot by the table. Big Eddy gripped the back of the chair and lifted him back into a sitting position. He began to untie his hands and feet from the chair.

"The balls on this guy, Bob, it'd be at least two

meals."

Bob said nothing to this.

"So you see the kind of unpleasantness that's possible, don't you, George? And what's more, I'd hate for your lovely girlfriend to be inconvenienced by this matter. What's her name? Gina? Works over at 'Curious Media' on Richmond. It'd be a hell of a shame to see that. So do we understand each other?"

"Perfectly." George looked the son-of-a-bitch right in the eyes and couldn't stop some of the anger from seeping out.

"I'm going to miss you, George," Eddy said as he bent down to undo the twine holding George's ankles to the chair. "All that shit about Hermes. Never take a drink. Always a bright spot in my day. I'm going to give you your hood back now. I wouldn't want you to be burdened with any additional information."

George nodded.

"My associates will drop you back downtown for your bike. But you have already worked your last day as a courier. Consider this your retirement party. Your pickups for the week will be handled by others. There will be no further need of your services."

"That's fine."

"Good-bye, George."

"Good-bye, Eddy."

His last view of Eddy was of him reaching up to put the sack over his head again and then darkness. He steeled himself for another blow or a punch, but nothing came. The door opened again and he was led out of the room and back to the van. He was pushed down face first to the floor again, which was okay by him. The less he knew the better. The van was started up and it reversed through the door and drove off.

It's amazing how much more comfortable you feel when you know your life is not in imminent danger, even tied up on the metal floor of a cargo van. He bounced happily along, so glad to have this thing finally over with that he didn't even mind the bump on the head. It was the absolute mildest of the possible outcomes he had imagined.

Briefly he wondered what misunderstanding made them think that Martin was investigating them. How confused were both parties to that call? He would have loved to have heard the exchange. Did they take his cell phone? No, he could feel it on his hip when he rolled to the right.

He wondered if he should feel worse that he was letting these guys off the hook. Here was a criminal operation that he knew about, and he wasn't planning to do his civic duty in the slightest. People would be getting away with immoral, criminal acts specifically due to his inaction. But he couldn't take the chance that something might happen to Gina. He didn't care what else happened. He wouldn't let anything hurt her. Besides, in a free society, why were drugs illegal, anyway? Because they were potentially harmful? Well, what about tobacco and alcohol? They're still for sale and the government makes a tidy little tax profit on the misery they create.

He was rationalizing already. The guilt must be

working on his subconscious. It was a moral choice, and not really a tough one at that. Maybe it should have been a more difficult decision for him. But maybe it's not the big moral choices we face in life, but the small ones that make the difference. Didn't small indiscretions, petty larceny, and insignificant untruths always have a way of snowballing? Looking the other way when someone puts a few extra envelopes in without re-weighing, cheating on your taxes, dealing drugs, murder... who was going to put the morality price tags on these acts? Was he just looking for a whiter shade of gray in all this?

But he couldn't help being deliriously happy now that today was the first day of the rest of his life with Gina, and all that other optimistic glass-is-half-full shit. He couldn't wait to tell her he'd quit, and all about his plans with Petey, the possibilities there, and promise her a better future. She deserved better. Big Eddy said he had balls, but he'd never even had balls enough to step up and be a man. Go after what he wanted instead of settling.

What had happened to him today was his secret, though. Just say he fell off the bike. Pothole. Hit his head. Simple. He didn't want her to be scared for him any more than she already was. And all she needed to know was that it was behind him. Behind both of them. He was stupid to have taken such risks. Arrogant. Lucky as hell to be riding back to his bike with nothing more than a bump on the head. Out of pocket on a pair of Ray-Bans, damn that Bob guy.

When he was finally back on the sidewalk next to

his bike, rubbing his sore wrists, it was almost 8:00pm. He quickly phoned to let Gina know he was coming straight home and had lots to tell her. Didn't want her to worry. He was on his way.

Cycling home was a strange feeling. He would miss the bike so much. It was the one good thing about the job he was giving up. Which was silly, because he could cycle any time he wanted. But it wouldn't be the same feeling: pure independence, exhilaration, the wind flowing all around him, the sheer aerodynamic thrill and the adrenaline pumping in his veins as he did battle with the traffic. The feeling that his bread and butter was right there, rolling along the road beneath him, something he could rely on.

A chapter in his life was coming to a close, and he was going to savor every block of the ride home.

The Trap

Dinner was a nuke-able entrée eaten out of a container in the kitchen. No beer tonight. He was going on a mission. He had to stake out a nuclear parts manufacturer and catch a couple of burglars in the act. Burglars who probably worked for an international arms dealer. Nope. It didn't get old no matter how many times he said it to himself.

His whole body was tingling in anticipation. The darkest outfit he could find was an old black track suit, which was a little ratty, but would suffice for this evening's activities. Because it could get cold depending on how long he had to wait, he had his winter coat just in case. They might not even come tonight. He had his cell phone, fully charged, a Thermos of coffee in a gym bag, and some chocolate bars. He didn't feel great about that, but he might need the sustenance.

Locking up his apartment, he cut a strange figure, all dressed in black with a parka and a gym bag. Might as well be a burglar himself in this get-up, he thought to himself on his way down the hall.

He took the elevator down to the parking garage,

started the Tercel and let it warm up for a couple of minutes. Lots of time, he figured. It was just after 8:00, so the factory had only closed an hour ago and it wouldn't be dark out for almost an hour.

Winding his way up the two levels of underground parking ramp, he emerged onto Finch Avenue and headed east. The radio was playing something melancholy. He searched for something more up-tempo. An oldies station was playing the Stones' *Start Me Up*, so he bopped along to that, feeling good. The song reminded him of the time just after he had graduated university. He had been glad to get the hell out at that point and very eager to start up his new career, The song had a special meaning for him. If only he had known that his start in insurance would stretch out into years of sameness, veering suddenly into this unlikely adventure.

When he came to Midland and turned left, instead of turning left again, towards Silver Star Boulevard, he took a right down a residential side street and parked his car there. He walked back across Midland and over to Kilcullen Castle Gate, the little side street off Silver Star where he and George had parked the time before. He walked along the front of an industrial plaza there which was closed for the evening, turned the corner and kept walking toward the next building.

In between the two structures was an alleyway which was not lit and which gave him a clear view of the end of Silver Star Boulevard and Ultimate Diecasting. He sat and leaned against the wall so he could monitor what went on over there, zipping up his parka as it was already a little chilly. The sun had gone down and the wind had picked up. Setting out his supplies for the evening, he poured himself a cup of coffee, milk and sugar already mixed in, and took a long sip.

The sky was almost dark and city lights spread out in all directions in the distance. It really was a massive, sprawling metropolis. Toronto had all seemed so huge and unknowable at first. He had moved here for a job and the city was so alien and impersonal to him. Once he had gotten to know the city, he realized that it was made up of many small villages and neighborhoods, each with an energy and identity and parking problems all their own. Little Italy, Chinatown, Greektown, The Annex, Bloor West Village... all these places had a unique character.

Best of all was the blessed anonymity. The feeling that he could go anywhere without fear of being recognized all the time by people who knew him in third grade. Or worse, high school. Here, he could keep himself to himself, something the big city buzz and hurry actually facilitated.

Now that he thought about it, the keeping to himself had begun around third grade. His mom had had a bad pregnancy when he was eight and there was a lot of whispered talk and *"What do we do about Martin?"* amongst the adults. His mom ended up in a prolonged stay in hospital on strict bed rest and Martin stayed with his Polish grandmother who spoke very little English. He had just learned to read, so he began doing a lot of that just to amuse himself. The quiet of the house and the stress on the adults' faces went away when he entered the realms of Prydain and Middle Earth.

When his mom came home from the hospital with no baby (and no womb, he later found out), the silence that descended on their house felt like the silent treatment he read about in the *Great Brain* books. Some kind of punishment he didn't understand. But whenever there were bad feelings at home, he could count on tapping into those good feelings that were always waiting inside the pages of a book. Escape, pleasure, and distraction were the friends and family he could count on.

So when other kids were having little brother problems, girlfriends and summer camp intrigues, he was reading about them in the Judy Blume books. All through high school, this pattern of reading for pleasure continued. After graduation, he had to get away from that house, choosing to go to university in Toronto. His love of reading stayed with him. His love for the anonymous life in the big city made his decision to make it his full-time home after he entered the working world.

Of course, he still made the weekly trek down the 401, west towards Kitchener, city of his birth. The weekly parental visit was as much a ritual as it was an act of will. As he was the only child of their union, he felt a responsibility to see his parents more often to compensate for the lack of other children, not to mention grandchildren, in their lives.

It certainly wasn't the pull of the town, which was a mostly student-infested rat's maze, surrounded by bland subdivisions forming a large, distended tumor on the hip of the Waterloo region. It was a working class town, which is what his parents were. His father worked in an auto plant from the time of their arrival in Canada until his recent retirement. His mother had worked as a clerk/typist in an insurance company nearby, which is how Martin got a job in the Toronto office of the same company when he was 23.

His beige Tercel had rolled into their driveway at 3:30pm the previous Saturday, the same time, give or take an hour, that he always arrived. Martin had hiked his overnight bag out of the passenger seat, closed and locked the door, and made his way up to the house.

"Hello, dear," said his Mom, always waiting at the door for him. "Come in, come in."

"Hi, Mom."

"Your father's downstairs, why don't you grab yourself a beer out of the fridge? I'm just making dinner."

Martin put his bag in the guest room and followed instructions, going directly to the fridge and grabbing himself a beer, which his belly could feel coming as soon as it was in his hand. Then it was down into the TV room to join his father in front of the set.

"Hi, Dad. What's on?"

His father looked up. "Hello, Martin. It's bowling right now."

"Who's winning?" He sat down and put his beer on a doily on the end table.

"Bert Henry, despite some tendinitis."

"Good show, Bert."

Martin sat quietly, drank his beer and forced himself to watch the parade of unspeakable human banality strutting across the screen. How he hated television.

His father was an expert indolent, and could sit in front of the TV for hours, drinking beer after beer. A lesser man would have become bored (as Martin did almost as soon as he sat down) and sought out other activities, but not his father. He was a man of deep concentration and studied indifference to the non-televised world around him. The heart attack was scheduled for 2-3 years after retirement, according to the statistical average. Martin watched the slow rise and fall of his father's chest and felt he could almost see it bubbling up beneath his rib cage as he sat there.

It had been forty years ago that a young, newly married immigrant couple stepped off the boat in the Toronto harbor to look out on this "New World" of opportunity. At that time, the Royal York Hotel was the tallest building in the Toronto skyline, and Martin often tried to imagine this vision of the city, and of his parents. Full of promise and vitality. In love. It was impossible to conceive of his parents ever having been in love, or showing a passion for anything, let alone for each other.

"Supper!" was the word that woke him. The beer buzz and the dull droning of the television set had quickly put him away, as usual. He and his father trudged up the stairs, leaving the television on mute, and seated themselves at the table. Pot roast, French fries, peas, and beer. His father intoned the grace and they all offered their solemn ratification of his words with their amens.

They ate, mostly in silence, but also occasionally his mother would encourage Martin to detail his week's activities, which were unremarkable at best. He told them about some of his co-workers and things he had heard about them, as well as some of his exchanges with brokers. They just nodded and chewed, and accepted each story as it was offered.

When it was over, he helped his mother clear the dinner dishes away to the kitchen.

"Delicious dinner, Mother," said his father.

"Yeah, Mom. That was great. What's for dessert?"

"We're going to have some chocolate cake, but you men can go downstairs while I do these dishes. I'll be down in a minute with the cake, and then we can eat in front of the TV. Hmm?"

"The cake sounds great, but I'd rather stab my own eyes with the fork than watch anymore fucking tel-uh-vision," is what he would have said if his private thoughts had happened to leak out of his mouth at that moment. Instead, he grabbed another beer, and it was once more into the breach.

After several televisual extravaganzae and a honkin' slice of choco-bliss, Martin's father was zonked out and snoring in a peaceful stupor. His mother sat knitting a sweater for who knows whom, half-watching the show. Martin got up and kissed her on the cheek and said, "Goodnight, Mom."

Away up to the guest room he stole, where he shed his clothes like an unwanted lizard skin, putting on pajamas and pulling out a paperback. It would be several hours till sleep overcame him, and then church, morning brunch and away home again to do laundry. Back in Toronto, out in the most faceless part of suburbia in a neighborhood of building block high-rises. What did that say about him? Had he never really embraced the "personality" of a neighborhood, or did the blandness of his choice indicate a deficiency in his own personality? What exactly was his life all about? Work, eat, read, sleep, parents on the weekend. This habit of keeping to himself was bordering on a hermit-like existence.

But here he was, living life on the edge all of a sudden. Attempting a makeover. Going out on a date. He was doing the work. The rest, he had to hope, would follow. He poured another coffee, and hugged his knees up to his chest for warmth. Should have brought a cushion.

The Rats Arrive

Dinner was finished, they were on their third cups of herbal tea and still George was talking. He was in fine form: wild plans, bold dreams, regrets, a bright future, and Gina just sat and took it all in.

"And I've already had some ideas about gazebos that echo various design motifs in residential building styles. That way the movement of the eye is not arrested, but flows smoothly over the whole backyard."

"I hope you're making notes about all this."

"For sure. I'm going to need to show all this to Pete on Sunday night. We're invited for dinner."

"All of a sudden? Did he check with Martha?"

"I don't know. It seemed spur of the moment."

"Maybe I should call her, see if we can bring something. I don't know what they're going to serve, but you remember the last time."

"Let's not go there."

"All right, but I'm not going to go hungry again."

"They'll probably barbecue," said George. "And we'll just bring some veggie burgs or dogs."

"That would work." She stood up and brought

both their mugs over to the sink and filled them with water. She ran a cloth over them and put them in the drying rack. "Well, it's pretty late, and some of us have to work in the morning."

"Yeah, you better get to sleep. I think I'll sit up and make some of those notes. I'm still pretty jazzed about the whole thing."

"Okay, baby." She kissed him on the forehead, and walked toward the bedroom, yawning as she went. "I expect you'll be making me breakfast in the morning, since you won't be working?"

"At your service, mi'lady."

She smiled. "Good night."

"Night."

He went into the living room and switched on the computer. Delayed e-mail, indeed. He wished he had been smart enough to think of that. But the bluff had worked. Or it was part of what worked. One desk lamp would do, he thought, so he went around and switched off all the other lights. Walking over to the bookshelf, he again surveyed his collection of architecture textbooks and folios of glossy photos, selecting three that he thought he would need, and returning to the desk.

Flipped through the first one, trying to get the feeling back, the old buzz of ideas flitting around in his mind. By the second text he was making notes and drawings on a sheet of paper.

His phone rang, and he jumped up quickly to prevent it from ringing a second time and waking Gina. "Hello?"

"Hello, George. It's Martin."

He walked down the hall to the kitchen and closed the door behind him. "Marty! I forgot about... How'd you do today?"

"Didn't you get my message?"

"No, sorry. I didn't even check my voice mail when I got home. What happened?"

"The call went really well. Better than I could've hoped."

"That's great. What did he say?"

"Oh, it was beautiful. At first he kept denying it all. Told me he was going to call the police. And I kept laying it on him."

"What'd you say?"

"I told him I was working with the cops, that I wasn't after him, just the big fish."

"Good one."

"I told him I would keep his name out of it if he co-operated. Said he didn't want his wife to read about him in the paper. Didn't want to see his kids only on visiting day. In jail! Well, I said the slammer, actually."

"You are evil!"

"I know. I felt a little guilty, but what the hell, this guy dug his own grave. And he probably would face charges."

"I'm sure he would. So then what happened?"

"Well, then he told me he was going to call his lawyer. So I say, 'Tom, we know all about you and Mr. Smith.' Use his first name all of a sudden, right? Total silence. Then he just cracked. Said he'd co-operate, do whatever I asked him to."

"Beautiful!"

"Yeah, and get this, you'll love this part. It turns out they had people in there from the FBI, snooping around."

"The FBI? Come on."

"No, really. He thought I knew this, I guess because I said I was working with the police. But it turns out the 'contract' they were working on was for the U.S. Department of Defense. Nuclear. So it looks like our boys are working for some international arms dealers."

"Marty, it sounds like you're getting in a little over your head here."

"I know. Isn't it exciting? I never would have believed that I'd get involved in this kind of thing. And it's all thanks to you."

George winced. "Yeah, that's great. It's been exciting. But I think it's time you handed everything over to the cops. Let them take it from here. Thank god you didn't go out there tonight."

"No, I did. I'm out here right now."

"Where?"

"Silver Star Boulevard. I'm on a stakeout. This is my cell phone. To call the cops with. Cool, eh?"

"Marty. Call the cops right now and get out of there. This isn't a game."

"No, wait. There's a car coming. And it's... a black Taurus. Unbelievable. These guys have no fear."

"Marty, get going right now. I'll call the cops for you."

"No, let's just see what they do. They're pulling their car around back again."

George couldn't believe what he was hearing. He was actually holding his breath, listening carefully in case he missed Martin's next words.

"Okay, now they're walking around to the front. What the hell? They're knocking on the door. Do you think they'll just smash in this time? Wait a second, someone's answering the door. It looks like a security — Oh my god, they shot him! They shot him, George!"

"Get the hell out of there, Martin! I'll call the police. Just run!"

He hung up the phone, ran out the back door and down the stairs three at a time. Hit the sidewalk running and pushing the buttons 9-1-1 as he ran in search of a cab.

"Emergency 9-1-1. What's your emergency?"

"I want to report a break-in in progress at 50 Silver Star Boulevard. A man's been shot. The burglars are there right now!"

"What's your name, sir?"

"Never mind that, get someone out there NOW! They shot a security guard. My friend is still there. He's in trouble."

"Okay, we have an officer en route. Where is your friend?"

"I don't know, but somewhere close by. He called me."

"We'll need to take statements from both of you, sir."

He hung up the phone. Breathing heavily, he stood looking at the phone for a second, then he ran back to the apartment, grabbed his jacket, locked the door on the way out, and ran back onto Bloor Street. He looked up and down and saw a cab about a block away heading towards him. He flagged it down, and jumped in the back when it pulled over.

"50 Silver Star Boulevard as fast as you can go."

Run

The sick feeling rose in Martin even as he was talking to George on the phone. The suddenness of it, the silence of it, just red instantly appearing on the gray shirt, and the body crumpling to the floor, and even then, the idea appearing in his mind: he had set this whole thing up. He had set up that poor security guard for death as surely as if he'd shot him himself. Widowed a woman he'd never met, perhaps orphaned his children. Didn't even check what new protection they might have brought in. Thought the whole thing was exciting, like cops and robbers. And now a man lay dead.

The nausea swelled up within him and found its way out. He fell over and vomited, coughing and spluttering. His stomach heaved again. He tried to choke it down, but it came up anyway. Again he coughed, and then he looked up at the building across the road only to see the man with the gun looking in his direction now. The man motioned inside the unit and started walking towards Martin. Martin's heart turned over in his chest.

He stood and ran down the alleyway in the dark.

* * *

The two men stood over the body of the felled security guard. The man with the gun removed the silencer.

"That was even easier than the alarm."

"Yeah, what an idiot. This whole profession is going downhill. There's no training anymore. Use to be you'd worry more about these guys than the effin' cops."

"I couldn't believe my eyes when he opened the door."

"You just wanna leave him here?"

"Yeah, there's — What the fuck was that?"

"Sounds like somebody pukin'."

"I see him. You get in there and blow that shitbox safe. I'll go check it out." He began walking, screwing the silencer back onto his gun.

The Chase

It felt like he was having a heart attack. Given the
shape he was in, that wasn't entirely out of the
question. He ran flat out down the alley and then
headlong around the corner without looking back.
He ran to the far end of the complex and paused to
look back. Not seeing anyone coming, he quickly
surveyed his surroundings.

A creek ran behind the buildings on the opposite
side of the street. Beyond that lay tracks for the GO
train. To his right, about a hundred yards away, was
Midland Avenue and traffic, lights, people, and his
car across the road. That was the obvious route and
he'd likely be cut off before he reached the road. He
ran in the direction of the creek, trying to stay low.

To reach the stream and double back behind Silver
Star Boulevard, he had to pass by the end unit
housing Ultimate Diecasting, where the other burglar
was inside right now finding out that he'd been
tricked and there was no new contract. How long that
would take him was anybody's guess.

Martin huffed and wheezed and kept on running.
Why hadn't he kept in shape? The most exercise he

got in an average week was carrying his groceries out to his car. His legs were on fire and his lungs were bursting. And it was so dark. He took a look behind him, trying to make out any movement in the half-moon's light.

Not seeing anything in front of him or behind him, he slowed to a walk, and kept to the back of the row of dark industrial units, praying that somebody would be working late. He could just as easily be running toward the gunman as away from him. The problem was, he didn't really know where the man was.

Coming to a gap between buildings, he peered around the corner. In the distance, he could see the lights of Midland Avenue, where he desperately wanted to be. He decided to risk a trip to the street front of the building to see what was going on.

He crept along beside the wall, keeping out of the light as much as possible. When he got to the front, he looked off to the right and peeked around the corner to the left. The man was jogging towards him along the front of the building. Martin turned tail and ran as fast as he could for the back of the building.

"Hold it right there, you fat fuck."

Martin froze. He was just ten feet away from safety.

"Turn around."

He slowly turned around to see the man holding the gun on him about thirty feet away from him. Martin shook all over, his heart pounding in his chest.

"Who do we have here?"

"J-just an underwriter."

"What the fuck is an 'underwriter?'"

"A paper-pusher. I was, um, out for a walk."

"Brought your cell phone, coffee, and chocolate for your walk, did ya? Nice try, Einstein. Why don't you come forward a little so I can see who I'm going to be wasting. I don't like to miss nothin'."

Martin walked forward a few steps into the light.

"Hey, don't I recuhnize you? From the hotel. You were the fat bastard on the elevator, went for chocolate on our floor. All right, what's going on?"

Before Martin could answer, the sound of a police siren cut through their conversation and some bright lights pointed in their direction. The thug took a quick look over his shoulder and locked back onto Martin.

"Freeze! Police! Drop your weapon."

Neither of them moved or even looked towards the light. Martin had to squint, now seeing the man only in silhouette.

"Mister Underwriter, I've already killed one stupid fuck tonight, one more ain't going to make a difference. You think I'm afraid to do hard time? Especially up here in Canada?" He looked over his shoulder.

Martin dove for the ground and rolled to his right as quickly as he could. Simultaneously, he heard the bullet hit the ground beside him and the *phish!* of the silencer, and then there were three quick shots. When he looked up, the man was on the ground and a female police officer pinned him under her knee. Martin's head was spinning, the blood was pounding in his ears, people were shouting, and the lights were flashing all around him. He closed his eyes just for a second, welcoming the blackness.

Shock

When George arrived in the taxi, the whole end of
the street was full of police cruisers and ambulances.
He paid the driver and got out of the car. He looked
around amongst all the confusion. Martin was
nowhere to be seen. Please, not the ambulances. He
walked towards the nearer of the two, but he was
stopped by a cop before he could see inside.

"Hey, you can't go back there."

"I'm looking for my friend, Martin."

"There's been a couple of shootings. I'm sure your
friend wouldn't have stuck around."

"Can you please check? I'm worried that he might
have been one of the ones shot. His name is Martin
Porchnik."

"Okay, wait here."

The cop wandered off, presumably in search of a
supervisor. George looked over at the place they had
parked only two nights ago, when all this had started.
So fucking stupid! He should've known better than
to take such risks, given his own situation. Which
was what made it so strange. It was hard to believe so
much had happened in a few days.

After a few more minutes, the cop returned.

"Yeah, I found your buddy Martin. C'mon. He's over here in an ambulance."

"Jesus! Is he okay?"

"He's fine. Just a little shook up. They're just questioning him now."

George followed him across the street and into the parking lot in front of number 50, where the ambulance had its doors open, and Martin sat on the tailgate with a blanket over his shoulders, talking to an older, broad-shouldered cop with an open notebook.

"Marty, how're you doing?"

"George, what are you doing here?"

"I came as soon as you called."

"Who are you, sir?" asked the cop.

"I'm the guy who called 911 after my friend, here, phoned me."

He frowned and looked at his notebook.

"We'll need a statement from you, also, sir."

"Yeah, no problem. How is he doing?"

"Your friend has answered most of our questions, but I'll ask you a few questions as well. I'll be back in a moment." He looked gravely at the two of them and then walked away towards the factory doors.

"You okay, Marty?"

"I feel like shit, actually."

"Did they get the two goons?"

"One shot dead, the other arrested." Martin briefly relayed the events of the evening to him in a deadpan voice. He looked like he had just woken up from a deep sleep, his hair all rumpled and his black tracksuit looking much like pajamas. He had a swipe of dirt up one side of his face.

"Wow! At least they got the guys. And they have you to thank for that."

Martin hung his head. "No, nobody should thank me for anything. I really screwed things up. That poor security guard guy. He's dead."

"That's not your fault."

"Isn't it?" said Martin, looking up at him. "I could've gone to the police. He'd still be alive if I did that."

"You couldn't have known how things would turn out."

"It's my fault. My stupidity led to this."

"Then it's partly my fault. I should never have got you started on this."

"But it was me who took it all the way. Probably because my own stupid life has been so dull and empty, I latched onto this excitement without really thinking about the consequences."

"Those guys said they still hadn't got what they came for. Odds are they would have come back again, and that same security guard would have been here either way, even without your phone call."

"Yes, and speaking of which. I didn't mention your involvement except to say that I phoned you. I told them I just staked this place out tonight because I knew about the file and had a feeling they'd hit it again. I also don't want to drag Tom Peterson into this when I gave him my word that he'd be off the hook if he co-operated."

Another moral choice, thought George. Martin had obviously found the gray area with which he was most comfortable, tried on the various sizes of morality and found one that fits. Catch the criminals, let the informant get away. Tell the partial truth, let the lies of necessity roll off his conscience. The big moral choice, and its consequences, would stay with him, but the little choices, and compromises, would just fade into the background.

When they were finished with the police and they had retrieved his cell phone, thermos and gym bag, George walked Martin over to his car.

"Little beige Tercel, oo-hoo, baby you're much too fast, yes you are," George sang mockingly.

"Knock it off," replied Martin, laughing in spite of himself. "Would you mind driving? I'm still a little shaky."

Martin opened the passenger side door and gave the keys to George. Martin made sure they both put on their seat belts and George started up the car and flipped it into drive without letting it warm up. The tires squealed a little bit as he hit the gas and accelerated over to Midland where he braked to an abrupt stop.

"I've got to warn you, I don't do a lot of driving, so I'm a bit of a wild man when I do."

"Go ahead, it'll seem like life in the slow lane compared to my day."

George turned toward home, taking it slow most of the way despite his threats.

"Yeah, we've both had quite a week, Marty. Did I tell you I quit my job today?"

"What? Why'd you do that?"

"I'm going into business with my brother. I hope. We're going to do landscape design, design-and-build decks and gazebos. It ain't architecture, but it's the poor cousin."

"That's fantastic, George. But we're going to miss your daily wisecracks at the office."

"You'll just have to pick up the slack."

They drove in silence for a while, George feeling as exhausted as Martin looked. In his big winter parka, ratty track-suit with puke stains on the front and his wild, disheveled hair, he looked like a refugee case.

"Will you miss being a courier?" said Martin. "I mean, I always knew you could do better, but you also seemed to be happy doing what you were doing."

"I was. And I will miss it. Not the low pay and the bastard cabbies and the potholes and the rain and the snide secretaries, but the good days, the fast rides, and anything to do with the bike, actually. I'm really going to miss the biking. Hey, speaking of which. You ever get out on two wheels?"

"Not much, no."

"Do you have a bike?" said George.

"Sure. At home in my parents' garage."

"Well, why don't you and I get together on weekends and do the bike riding thing? It'd be great exercise, and then we won't be able to make excuses as easily. Like the buddy system. What do you say to that?"

"Yes. I almost burst a lung running away from that gun-toting thug today. I need the exercise."

"Excellent. When do we begin?"

"It'll have to be Sunday," said Martin. "I'll be staying over at my parents' house on Saturday, but I'm usually back by Sunday at lunchtime. I'll give you a call."

"Perfect. And why don't you come for dinner afterward? I'd like you to meet Gina. I'll whip you up a vegetarian meal."

"Done. By the way, I've got a date tomorrow night."

George looked at him with surprise. "What? With who?"

"Janice."

"I can see that. She's one of the nice ones and quite the cutie. Did you ask her or did she ask you?"

"I asked her."

"That's great news, Marty! You are coming out of your shell. Good for you."

"I'm not sure that's a compliment."

George laughed. "Unless you're a turtle. No, I'm really happy for you. That's very exciting."

They locked up the car in the underground parking and took the elevator up to the lobby, where they both got off.

"Thanks a lot for driving," said Martin. "I really wasn't up to it."

"Not a problem. You take it easy. You going in to work tomorrow?"

"Oh, yeah. Wouldn't miss it."

"Okay, well, call me Sunday. We're over in Bloor West Village, so you can just drive your bike over in your car and we can go from there."

"Sure thing. Talk to you tomorrow. You going to be okay getting home?"

"Yeah, I'll just get a cab."

Martin looked at him. "Your arch-nemesis?"

"Hey, if you can't beat 'em." George smiled and held up his hand for a fist bump.

Consequences

The alarm, a splitting headache, and a body that was sore all over woke Martin up at the usual time the next morning. At least he was able to switch off the alarm, although even that movement was painful. Coffee and headache pills were immediately required. He flicked on the coffeemaker and headed straight for the shower.

With no stomach for breakfast, he just had the coffee and painkillers and headed out early for the subway. It was busier than usual because he was leaving slightly earlier, so he had to stand. The hot shower had helped his aching muscles and he had stretched enough of them when putting on his clothes that the pain had mostly subsided. The headache remained, due in no small part to the guilt he felt. Nothing more painful than a guilty conscience.

The train squealed and rumbled along underground all the way down to Eglinton, where it briefly surfaced to give them a look at the Mount Pleasant Cemetery, which was positively *verdant* in the early morning sunlight. Strange to think that such a beautiful place could serve such a sombre purpose.

After the brief glimpse of daylight and greenery, the train turned its nose downward, and they descended once more into the dark.

The vision of the security guard opening the door, the blood springing onto his shirt, and then his limp collapse to the floor was one which he was not able to switch off. It had invaded his subconscious in dreams and it played itself over and over in his mind whenever his concentration wandered for a second. Due to his mistake, his miscalculation. He needed to do better.

The world of crime had always seemed so glamorous and exciting when he read about all those detectives and villains, cops and robbers, shootings and car chases, interrogations and smart aleck replies. And the occasional innocent bystander getting killed just heightened the determination to solve the case and get the bad guy. It was all so utterly divorced from the reality he now knew as to be absurd to him. He knew that he would never be able to read and enjoy another of those books again. That left westerns and war novels. And other stuff, surely. What else was out there?

The elevator door opened on the 46th floor and he stood for a moment before he realized it was his floor. He caught the door as it was closing, it opened again, and he stepped out into the hallway to many a disgusted look from the crowd. No delays allowed! Anger welled up in him all of a sudden.

"Well, excuse the fuck out of me! So sorry you'll all be six seconds late for work!"

The people all looked shocked and horrified. Someone had spoken to them on an elevator! Two people quickly pressed the *Door Close* button to get away from this freak. The doors shut on the scene of harried nine-to-fivers looking worriedly at each other, as if noticing for the first time that there were other passengers in the car next to them.

Martin felt much better for having said this and he walked into the office with a little more bounce in his step.

"Good morning, Janice."

"Good morning, Martin. How are you?"

"Surviving."

"Oh, I hope your day gets better."

"I think it will… at around 7:00 tonight." He smiled at her in a mischievous way and she beamed back at him with obvious pleasure.

He put his lunch in the fridge and poured himself another coffee before walking over to the cube. Preemptive good mornings all around, greeting Dave and Darlene before they greeted him, and warning Dave that he'd be babbling any second now. He switched on his computer and went right into his calendar for the word of the day:

Frondescent - *(frond-e-sent)* a. Springing into leaf; expanding into fronds.

"It was a beautiful spring day, and all the trees in the valley were frondescent in the bright sunshine."

A familiar voice came from behind the cubicle wall. "How poetic."

"Thank-you, Dave."

He looked around at his cubicle. Saw all the files that had piled up, correspondence waiting for reply, quotes waiting to be quoted. It was clear that his mind hadn't been on his job over the last couple of days. Why did the desk seem so much smaller today? Something clicked in his mind and he decided to pay Gerry a visit.

"Yes, Martin? What can I do for you?"

"Gerry, I'd like to talk about my future prospects with the company."

"Sit down. What do you mean, future prospects?"

Martin sat in the chair across from her. "I'd like to change my career focus to investigations and loss control."

She looked at him for a second, her face showing her surprise. "When did you come up with this plan?"

"I think it's just time for a change and it's an area that interests me. Why is that surprising?"

"Martin, you have sat in the same desk for 15 years. You've been here longer than me and everyone else in the department. You've never mentioned anything like this before."

He reflected on that and nodded. "I guess so."

"Well, I don't have any loss control positions available right now, but it's good to know you're interested. With your knowledge of commercial policies, you'd probably be really valuable working on Commercial Property claims."

"Yeah," said Martin. "That sounds promising, too. Let me think about it."

"I'll let H.R. know that you're thinking about a move, and to let us know if something comes open. Meanwhile, don't piss off the people in Admin. And watch for any internal postings in the staff room."

"Thanks a lot. I'll keep my eyes open."

"What am I going to do without my Senior Underwriter?"

He returned to his desk to try to make some headway into the backlog, but the phone kept ringing. People kept coming up with problems, either claims files or an opinion on a quote. It was one of those mornings when interruptions conspire to keep you from your work, when you could least afford it. It was just one more phone call, just before noon.

"Hello, Martin Porchnik speaking."

"Good morning. I wanted to call to thank you for your recent assistance."

"Who is this?"

"You helped to rid me of my two bothersome associates with little or no vexation on my part, and for that you have my gratitude."

"Mr. Smith?"

"Sometimes."

"How did you—"

"How did I obtain your name? I spoke to my good friend Tom Peterson. I can be very persuasive. And, as I said, I really had to thank you."

The nerve of this guy, thought Martin. "Well, at least you didn't get what you needed."

"No, and that is regrettable. But I have already found an alternate source for the missing information, which may prove to be even more fruitful than this one in the long run."

"You won't get away with it. Your 'associate' probably gave your name to the police right away when he was arrested. The one who lived, I mean."

"I am certain he did. But I was checking out of the hotel and discarding my former identity even as they were on their way to be caught in your little trap."

"You knew about that?"

"Oh, yes. I thought it was brilliant. I played along, of course."

"I have call display, you know."

"I really don't think your call display will be of much use in tracking my disposable mobile phone in a moving vehicle."

"So what do you want from me?"

"I want to know why you did all this. I want to understand you."

"Why do you care?"

"In my line of work, you never know who your opponent will be. But I never thought it would be an insurance clerk with a grudge."

"First of all, I'm not a clerk, I'm an Underwriter. And it wasn't a grudge. The file was forced on me, but it had my name on it, and it just didn't add up. I couldn't just leave it, for some reason. I don't know why. There have been lots of losses before, but not like this one. I had to make sure the guys who pulled this one were caught."

"You see, that just fascinates me. It was highly entertaining watching you work."

"Well, I'm so glad I can be your entertainment. I've been beating myself up for that security guard's death, but really, that's on you. You were the instrument behind all of this. And I promise you, I'm going to make sure that you get caught."

"Mr. Porchnik, I am certain that you must feel very insulated from me. Very safe. As though there is no way I could touch you, way up there on the 46th floor, sitting in your cubicle wearing that unfortunate brown-striped tie."

Martin looked down at his chest and then turned to look out the window behind him. *How in the hell?*

"Be glad that you amuse me. Good day to you, sir."

Martin hung up the phone feeling absolutely numb. He had no fear left. Let him do his worst. It was no more than he deserved. Did Mike Hammer ever let the bad guy get away? That would be a definite character flaw. Oh, well. At least he got two of them. And maybe this would be the beginning of his detective career. He was smart and had great intuition for when he wasn't getting the whole story. Maybe if he worked on these skills he could help put a few more goons behind bars. Who knows? If he was really lucky, maybe he would get another shot at Mr. Smith some day. And next time, he'd be ready.

Risk

--

About the Author

Happily married since 1992 and a father since 2003, Mark has been a writer for as long as he can remember. He was born in Toronto and grew up in London, Canada. He was the first winner of the *Lillian Kroll Prize for Creative Writing* at Western University, where he also completed a degree in English Literature. The manuscript for *Risk* was a semi-finalist in the *Chapters Robertson Davies First Novel Contest* and it cracked the Top Ten *Mystery/Thriller Hot List* on *Wattpad.com* in the summer of 2014. Mark has published novels, poetry, short fiction, feature articles, comic strips and book reviews in various media.

He lives in London with his wife and daughter, those to whom all his work and play is dedicated.

Connect with Mark - http://markvictoryoung.com/

Risk

Also from *Hanton House* by Mark Victor Young
Once Were Friends - a Novel

If you think it's hard to win back the one that got away, try doing it while you're taking over her family's company.

To save the firm his father built, ambitious CEO Hal Mercer has to initiate a hostile takeover of industry giant D'Arville Industries.

Owned by the family of the only woman he's ever loved, Kate certainly isn't going to stand by and let him destroy her family's empire. If only she'd have dinner with him, he could make her understand his intentions. If Hal fails, it's his family's company that's doomed, his employees who'll lose their jobs. He can't let that happen, but Hal isn't used to having everyone counting on him like this.

Problem is, it's becoming less clear which is more important to him—winning the corporate battle of his life or the heart of the woman he loves.

Sample First Chapter

They were pinned down under heavy fire in the empty shell of what had looked like a partially burned-out general store. Hal Mercer crouched below a windowless frame on the second floor, listening for footsteps on the stairs. Damn! Now his mask was fogging up. He tried to wipe it with one finger, hearing shouts in the smoky air as the enemy crawled up their unprotected flank, the heavy *Phut! Phut! Phut!* of sniper fire covering their approach. Where the hell did he go from here?

Hal glanced out the window. Abandoned car wrecks covered with spray paint lined the street in front of the building, stacks of tires lay toppled at the curb, obscure suggestions of movement over there told him that enemy positions were advancing along the tree line to his right, and then the sound of two slugs slamming into the window frame next to his ear made him duck back under the ledge. Raising his gun over the ledge for a moment, he squeezed off a round in the general direction of the trees.

"Archie?" he shouted off into the darkness to his left.

"Yes, mon capitaine?"

"You see those guys coming up by the trees?"

A pause. "Yes, sir."

"Can you create a diversion on your side to draw their fire?"

"I'm on the case, sir."

Archie was playing some kind of game, obviously. He wasn't this good at taking orders and he also hated Hal intensely. He would be more likely to stab Hal in the back than cover it for him.

"Go ahead, then," Hal yelled.

Then a shuffling noise from the next room and several shots followed by a wet *SLAP*, and Archie Bishop's voice shouting, "I'm hit, I'm hit! They got me, captain!"

Hal's heart was pounding in his chest as he reviewed his options. With Archie out, he was likely all alone here on the second floor, with who knew how many of his division gone. Going outside would be suicide, as he could see from the figures advancing on all sides, but staying here only delayed the inevitable.

Then there was a squeak from behind him, and the sound of a careful footstep on the stairs, and Hal, keeping low under the window, crawled to the darkened corner at the far end of the room, his weapon pointed at the top of the stairs. The dark shape of a head bobbed into view, eyes trained along the barrel of a gun that scanned left and right like a periscope on an emerging submarine. Then more of the body came into view: an absurdly tall, hunched-over figure with sticking-out ears and ridiculous fatigues—it was Johnson from Accounting.

"Die, pencil-pusher," said Hal as he squeezed the trigger, firing a single round into Johnson's midsection.

"Ow!" said Johnson. "I'm hit."

The adrenaline rush was amazing! Oh, well. Nothing left to lose. Hal scurried to the window and started firing at anything and everything that moved. "Banzai! This one's for Archie." He caught someone hurrying across the street in front of him and quickly fired a couple of rounds in that direction. A woman's voice called out, "I'm hit," just as he caught sight of the tiny yellow orb coming at him, seemingly growing larger as it descended along its shallow arc, and exploding on contact with his visor. Shaking his head from the surprising force of the impact, he couldn't quite shake off the darkness of the thick paint obscuring his view.

Hal shouted, "I'm hit," and sank back blindly onto the floor to wait for the whistle. He had been killed yet again, but he couldn't help smiling. Who knows what it was doing for morale, but he was having the most fun he'd had in ages. Why had it taken him so long to discover the joy of paint ball? He felt good about the way the Senior Management team rallied around him, even if they had lost two of their three engagements. What the heck, at worst it was something different for everyone to do on a weekend that was on the company tab.

Okay, sure, he wasn't that "easy come, easy go" about it. He had spent weeks planning this event and was desperately hoping everyone was having fun. And morale simply had to improve; it couldn't get much worse. It was a tough time for the company now and if he was going to achieve what he wanted—

no, scratch that—what he had to achieve, then he had to make some changes for the better.

Was he the only one who worried about this stuff? Right. Sniff, sniff. It's lonely at the top.

* * *

"Okay, troops. Let's bring it in," said Bill Fluellen, the section manager, as they were milling around in the lobby. Pete Malden rolled his eyes. Another management speech. Didn't he get enough of this during the work week? He looked over at Fluellen. His boss was an imposing figure even when he wasn't dressed in military fatigues. His thick red hair and salt and paprika goatee was flecked with sweat and sawdust.

"We did great out there," he was saying. "We worked together and really stuck it to those wallies from the IT crew. Malden and Bardolph, way to cover each other. Where's Bardolph?"

"Right here, sir. Ten-hut!" Randy Bardolph snapped to attention behind his boss in a mock salute.

"At ease. You were quite the drama queen with your little 'death scene' out there."

"Sorry, sir. Next time I give up my life for you in battle, I'll try to go with more dignity."

"Excellent. Bottom line, we came together as a team and defended our position despite overwhelming odds. As your commanding officer, I was damn proud to lead you onto the field. That's the last exercise of the day, so I'll just say enjoy the rest of your weekend, and I'll see you back at the office Monday morning."

Pete sat on a low bench against the wall and covered his nose with his sleeve as the pervasive combined aroma of stale sweat, cigar smoke and something moldy mingled with the fresh body odors filling the room. Randy, Amy, and Arthur sat or stood next to him.

"Pete, I love the blue hair," said Amy, smoothing her own hair behind both ears with her fingertips. "You should really keep it like that." Her dark hair was in a short bob kept away from her face. She had a mostly slim and petite frame, so her navy sweatshirt with the George Brown College logo hung a bit too loosely from her shoulders, but her curvy hips filled out her dark olive army pants so she didn't just look skinny.

He liked being able to see this casual side of her. Even on dress down day she wasn't like this, preferring business casual to jeans and a T-shirt. Those army pants were driving him wild. He wondered if they could somehow make paint ball a weekly thing.

Pete caught her eye and then ran his fingers through the blue patch of hair and looked away. "Yeah, thanks. My version of a battle scar. 'It's a far better thing I do than I have ever done', one life to give for the department and all that."

"So what are we supposed to feel now? A stronger

sense of team cohesion?" said Randy. "Or do you find yourself with even more questions about the people you work with?"

"Yeah," said Arthur. "Like what was with those IT geeks who had their own guns?"

"Scary," said Pete. "And some were like automatics or something."

"I have a picture in my mind," said Randy, applying two fingers to his right temple and closing his eyes, his mouth pursed in a little smirk. He was what you might call portly, but with a dignified air and busy hands with long fingers that were animated when he talked and drumming or tapping when he was listening. He cleared his throat. "They are here every weekend, keeping track of their 'kill-shots,' have a full set of military fatigues—no offence, Amy —have no girlfriends, live in their parents' basements which smell exactly like this place, and they're each composing the ultimate online game to ensure their places in history."

Amy put a hand on her hip. "The only reason I have these army pants is because they were in fashion for about 10 minutes when I was in grade 12, and this is the only place I've had a chance to wear them since then, and when's the last time you had a girlfriend, Randy?"

"Touché," said Randy.

"I think you make a cute military chick," said Pete.

"Thank-you, Peter." She smiled at him.

"Yeah, I was going to say that, too, Amy," said Arthur. "I noticed the same thing."

Pete looked at his rival. Shit, that's all he needed. Not that Arthur was much competition. He was tall and thin with a generally hunched posture that looked a bit like he was trying to brace himself for impact. Inexplicably, he was wearing a blue oxford cloth button down and beige cotton chinos, as if he were off to a college mixer of yesteryear, albeit they were now tie-dyed with paint splotches. Did they have college mixers in the Summer of Love?

Amy gave Arthur a suspicious look. "There's no way I'm doing your reconciliation for you next week so you can forget it."

"No, I wouldn't, I just…" said Arthur.

Randy patted Arthur on the shoulder. "Of course you wouldn't, Arthur. Did anybody catch sight of our fearless leader? He was supposed to be here today."

"Hal? No, but I would love to know who shot him," said Pete.

"We'll hear about it Monday, I'm sure," said Amy.

"I'm surprised we didn't get a speech from the little general," said Randy.

"Which unit just squared off with the S&M team?" asked Arthur, using their secret code for the Senior Management group.

"I think it was Marketing, and you know they'd lie down and play dead rather than smoke the big bosses," said Pete, leaning back against the wall and folding his arms across his chest. "They know which side their bread is buttered." He had a slim build and wore black jeans and a long sleeve red t-shirt with a

Spider-Man symbol surrounded by webs on the front. His blue eyes and long lashes were the occasional envy of the women in his life, but his normally dark and not blue hair was short and messy-on-purpose.

"They're smart. You've got to learn to play politics with the management types if you ever want to become one." Amy made a nose plugging gesture and craned her neck to see over the crowd. "Geez, it smells. Is that line getting any shorter? I'd really like to get out of here."

"I know," said Pete. "I feel like the smell is in my mouth now. I might just need a cold beer to counteract it."

* * *

"So whose idea was it to do this whole team-building paint ball thing, anyway?" said Arthur as they sat around a table at *The Fletcher's Quiver* Pub. They had a booth to the right of the bar, slightly toward the back. Pete surveyed the room and the various Robin Hood artifacts above their heads.

"Well, what else can you think of that's new around the office?" said Randy.

"Yeah, I know Hal is the new CEO, but do you really think it was his idea?"

"Of course it is. When you're the new guy, you have to come in and piss on the bushes, mark your territory," said Randy. "This is just one of many new things still to come, and not all of them will be good, just wait."

"But it was his father's company," said Arthur. "Why would he want to change things so much? I mean, doesn't that reflect poorly on his dad?"

"More likely he wants it to reflect well on him," said Pete.

"Yes, our boy does have a reputation to live down," said Randy. "He was the biggest shit disturber of all of us when he worked the floor with Pete and me."

"Wow," said Arthur.

Randy and Pete exchanged an uncomfortable glance, remembering somebody was missing. A year earlier, they would have been here with Hal, talking about the very people he was probably out for drinks with right now.

Thursday nights after work were what Hal had dubbed "group therapy" sessions at the local watering hole. There were always five to ten of them from the office, a revolving door of old pros, new hires who looked promising and the core group of Hal, Pete and Randy. Hal would get Randy going about something and then he would hold court while Hal bought a round of *B-52s* or *Sexes on the Beach* or something and hit on the waitresses. Pete would draw pictures of the senior managers or supervisors and they would end up eating chicken wings for their dinner around 10 o'clock and then close out the bar. Pete and Randy would stumble onto the subway and Hal would grab a taxi going the other way, often with female companionship in tow.

For about the last six months it had been just Pete and Randy. After Arthur had joined their section, he had come out once in a while, but their get-togethers had become less frequent since Hal had ascended the top of the org chart. The dynamic was somewhat flat without him.

"Yeah," said Pete. "And before he surprised everyone and came to work with us, he did the whole life of leisure, rich kid, country club. We heard all the stories, believe me."

Randy nodded agreement while he finished a sip of his martini. "My uncle golfed at his club and knew him well. Hal would spend all day on the golf course. An excellent golfer, I'm told."

"I'll bet he was a hit with the ladies," said Amy. "With that rock star hair and those dark eyes... mmm, yummy."

"You have a woody for our CEO?" said Pete. "Ewww. Now I know how you plan to get to the top."

"He can heighten my, um, future prospects any time." Amy smiled at all of them.

"Quite," said Randy. "But you notice the rock star hair was gone before the board meeting when they voted on his coronation? And he actually went out and bought his first suit. Our boy Hal has really grown up."

"I'm sure he had his suit and haircut before the funeral," said Pete. The others all nodded and found it was a good time to have a sip of their drinks and inspect their surroundings. Pete looked down at the Robin Hood caricature he'd been doodling on a spare bar mat, picked it up and shook it to dry the ink. "But I'll give you this: he was the laziest one of any of us on the fifteenth floor."

"Hear, hear," said Randy. He looked at his watch. "Well, I think it's time I moved on. Do you still need a ride?" He touched Arthur's arm.

"Yeah," said Arthur, sucking back the last of his beer.

Randy indicated the half full glasses in front of them. "Are you guys staying on?"

"I'm just going to finish this beer," said Pete.

"Me, too," said Amy.

"Right. See you Monday." Randy waved and walked to the front door and out, followed closely by Arthur.

Pete smiled and had a casual sip of his drink. "Sorry, I didn't mean to break up the party."

"You didn't," said Amy. "It was just one of those pauses in the conversation. And I think Randy was realizing he sounded a little full of himself."

"Doesn't he always?"

"Let's see how you're coming along with Robin Hood. Hey, pretty good likeness of Hal, there. Is he an anti-Robin? The rich stealing from the poor?"

"Isn't that what the rich always do? No, I just felt like putting his head on a Robin Hood body. Inspired by my surroundings."

Amy nodded. "It's really good."

"Thanks. So what did you think of today, really?"

"I liked it. As corny as it sounds, it does build team spirit. It lets us have a little fun and see a different side of the people we work with, and I would never have tried it otherwise."

"Yeah, I guess so. But requiring us to give up most of our Saturday for a work function kinda bugs me."

"I work plenty of Saturdays as it is."

"Yeah, but that's different. It's voluntary. I don't know, it just rubs me the wrong way. Do I really want to socialize with the people I work with? Don't I see them enough with, what, 45% of my waking hours spent at work already?"

"Should I be offended?"

"I didn't mean you, and you know it."

"Hey, you could've got a doctor's note."

"I know. Ignore me, I'm just lipping off. So what do you have planned for tonight? Any hot date on the horizon?"

"A hot date with my laundry is all."

"What, no boyfriend for the great Amy Quick, after giving Randy a hard time this afternoon over his lack of female companionship?"

"I don't think Randy craves female companionship. And no, neither of us has a boyfriend."

"Whaaat? You think Randy's gay? Just because he doesn't have a girlfriend? Does that make me gay, too?"

"No, with you I can't see it. But Randy has a quality, as they say." She paused and looked towards the door. "He never really talks about his social life, does he?"

"I, let me think… Who did he go on vacation with that time? Down south?"

"My point exactly. A friend is all he said."

"All right, maybe. I don't know. So what if he is?"

"I just like to ride him a little bit. See if I can shake his unflappable reserve."

"But you're not going to cause any embarrassing scenes? I prefer 'don't ask, don't tell,' if we could just keep it at that."

"Oh, I'm not going to out him, don't worry. Now what have you drawn there?"

"Oh, this." He shook the bar mat dry again and showed her the second figure.

She took it and peered at it while holding it to face the light. "What is that? Is that Randy as a cat?"

"That's Randy as a player in Cats."

"Oh, I get it. A Broadway musical." She smiled and put it back down on the table.

"Yes, I guess you've poisoned my mind now, and I will never be able to think of him without thinking that."

"You know what they say about homophobes…"

"No, I don't. And I don't want to know. Not that I think that way. I'm fine with it."

Amy nodded and sipped her drink down to the ice cubes.

"So what happened with, I think his name was Joey, or Joe?"

"What?"

"The old boyfriend? Now no longer."

"Oh, yeah. Well, I guess we were both so busy with

work, we were just seeing each other less and less. I'm still doing the night school classes, so it was hard to even get a free night that we could get together. So I said let's quit it and save ourselves a painful break-up."

"Right. That's grounds for a painful break-up right there."

"He was okay. Relieved, almost. We both realized it wasn't going anywhere, I think."

"You think."

"You don't know Joe. He works longer hours than I do."

"Mmm."

"Well, it's getting to be that time." She looked around for a clock. "My dirty clothes beckon."

"Yeah, I guess I'll get going, too. Where are you parked?" He shimmied down to the end of the bench and stood.

"Right out front," she said, standing. "Where are you?"

"Not far." They walked around the front of the bar and out the main door to the sidewalk. Pete pointed back down the road towards the *Paint War!* building. "Back the way we came. About a block back, there. The red one."

"Okay, well, see you Monday." She smiled and squinted into the light.

"See you Monday. Right." He did a sort of wave, and half turned towards his car.

Amy produced a key fob from her purse and aimed it at a car, pressing a button that made the car's lights flash. She walked around to the driver's side and opened the door. "Bye."

He nodded. "Bye."

Pete walked down the sidewalk towards his car, not looking back in case she was watching to see if he looked back. No more boyfriend. This was fantastic. He hadn't lied about her military outfit—he was hot for her in those clothes. He had, of course, always noticed her tight little body and always felt a bit of the tease in the way she looked at him and talked to him. Now that there was no boyfriend in the picture, it was all about strategy. Time to make his move. He would have to deal with Arthur, of course, but that would wait until Monday.

It was a cool fall day, slightly overcast. He drove home with the windows down and his music turned up, smiling at nothing. Home was a one-bedroom apartment in the Danforth, Toronto's Greektown area. It was sparsely furnished, had a cabinet full of movies, and everywhere boxes and boxes of comics. Various framed superhero posters by his favorite artists decorated the walls.

The kitchen table was also his drawing board for his own drawings, most of which were of the superhero or heroine variety. His Saturday night consisted of a heated can of ravioli eaten at the table while working on a large-scale Batman scene, with the original Batman movie, the one with Jack Nicholson as The Joker, playing in the background for atmosphere.

There used to be more furniture, and some throw

pillows, and tasteful decorative prints on the walls, and no room for any of his things in the bathroom, but that stuff had been gone for some time now. Now there was more room for his comics, and he could leave the boxes all over the place and no one complained.

At the same time, he missed the other stuff.

For further details or to purchase a copy of *Once Were Friends,* please visit http://markvictoryoung.com/once-were-friends/

Praise for Mark Victor Young's writing:

"Solid writing with great dialogue and interesting characters!" – Bruce Elgin

"This is the type of book I go to when I want to unwind and forget the world." – Lucy Butler

"That voice makes us curious and keeps us reading." – Cynthia Dagnal-Myron

"A novel which moves along very nicely and captures my attention." – Ann Elizabeth Carson, author of *We all become stories*

Coming soon from Mark Victor Young
Award-winning author of *Once Were Friends*

Awkward Stages - *A book of short stories* - A girl and boy discover the difference between "Best Friends" and just friends. The summer before university is the catalyst for some strange longings. A woman wrestles with a difficult insurance claim which resonates with an event from her past. An aging writer gives a career-spanning interview with an unintended revelation. These and other great characters inhabit this collection of short stories which celebrate all of life's stages.

Praise for the stories:

"There are so many good things in this story it's hard to pick one. All I can say is I wish I had written it." - Charles Pinch

"Thanks for this potent kick of nostalgia. How important those days were to the adults we've become. Call that 'The High School Theory.'" - Beverly Akerman, author of *The Meaning of Children*

A note on Copyright and Licensing

This novel is distributed under a **Creative Commons Attribution - NonCommercial - NoDerivatives 4.0 International (CC BY-NC-ND 4.0)** License. That means:

You are free to:

Share — copy and redistribute the material in any medium or format

The licensor cannot revoke these freedoms as long as you follow the license terms.

Under the following terms:

Attribution — You must give appropriate credit, provide a link to the license, and indicate if changes were made. You may do so in any reasonable manner, but not in any way that suggests the licensor endorses you or your use.

Non-Commercial — You may not use the material

for commercial purposes.

No Derivatives — If you remix, transform, or build upon the material, you may not distribute the modified material.

No additional restrictions — You may not apply legal terms or technological measures that legally restrict others from doing anything the license permits.

Notices:

You do not have to comply with the license for elements of the material in the public domain or where your use is permitted by an applicable exception or limitation.

No warranties are given. The license may not give you all of the permissions necessary for your intended use. For example, other rights such as publicity, privacy, or moral rights may limit how you use the material.

For any reuse or distribution, you must make clear to others the license terms of this work. The best way to do this is with a link: http://markvictoryoung.com/

Any of the above conditions can be waived if you get permission.

Full legal text available here:
http://markvictoryoung.com/cc-by-nc-nd-4-0/

More info about Creative Commons here:
http://creativecommons.org